STORIES WITHOUT END
TAYLOR SAPP

OTHER BOOKS BY ALPHABET PUBLISHING

SUCCESSFUL GROUP WORK — *13 Activities to Teach Teamwork Skills*
Patrice Palmer

CLASSROOM COMMUNITY BUILDERS — *Activities for the First Day and Beyond*
Walton Burns

KEEPING THE ESSENCE IN SIGHT — *From Practice and Observation to Reflection and Back Again* (forthcoming)
Sharon Hartle

50 ACTIVITIES FOR THE FIRST DAY OF SCHOOL
Walton Burns

Integrated Skills Through Drama Series

HER OWN WORST ENEMY — *A serious comedy about choosing a career*
Alice Savage

ONLY THE BEST INTENTIONS — *A modern romance between a guy, a girl, and a game*
Alice Savage

RISING WATER (Forthcoming) — *A stormy drama about being out of control*
Alice Savage

We are a small, independent publishing company that specializes in resources for teachers in the area of English language learning. We believe that a good teacher is resourceful, with a well-stocked toolkit full of ways to elicit, explain, guide, review, encourage, and inspire. We help stock that teacher toolkit by providing teachers with practical, useful, and creative materials.

Sign up for our mailing list on our website, www.alphabetpublishingbooks.com, for announcements about new books, and for discounts and giveaways you won't find anywhere else.

STORIES
without
END

24 open-ended stories to engage students
in reading, discussion, and creative writing

Taylor Sapp

ISBN   978-1-948492-11-9

Library of Congress Control Number: 2018935996

Country of Manufacture Specified on the Last Page

First Printing 2018

Published by:
Alphabet Publishing
1204 Main Street #172
Branford, Connecticut 06405 USA

info@alphabetpublishingbooks.com
www.alphabetpublishingbooks.com

Designed by Annabel Brandon

All images from DepositPhoto and Adobestock except "Jack and the Beanstalk" page 24 by Warwick Goble (Public Domain). Author's photo taken by Taylor Sapp.

Dedication

Special thanks should also be given to friends, family, teachers, and students who helped in the reading and testing of these stories!

Abdulaziz Albatli

Mona Alfayez

Sima Mansour Almashaf

Abdulelah Alsaed

Hussam Aljumah

Hanan Alrabiee

Rasheed Alrabiee

Ahmed Alrashed

Turki Althaqib

Juan Camilo Arieza-Lopez

Cassie Chia-Chi Chang

Wei Ling Chang

Katrina Cui

Ayumi Funakawa

Mina Gavell

Ryo Hatakeyama

Noriki Honsako

Seichiro Hori

Suzuna Kiso

Moeka Kudo

Peter Lacey

Andrew Lawrence

Atsushi Nakamura

Yui Okabe

Honoka Sato

Yurie Sato

Rika Yasukawa

My excellent publisher and editor, Walton Burns

And, of course, my family, Aya, Quinn, Noah, Susan, Parker, James and Leslie

TABLE OF CONTENTS

How to use this Collection —————————————————————————— VIII

PART I:

Short Takes (UNDER 500 WORDS)

1. Choose a Path ———————————————————————————————— 1

2. Family Matters ———————————————————————————————— 5

3. The Lunch of the Twelve ————————————————————————— 8

4. The Glass is Half . . . ——————————————————————————— 13

5. Pick a Pet ——————————————————————————————————— 17

6. Gifted —— 20

7. Joe and his Beans ———————————————————————————— 24

8. The Eyes Have It ———————————————————————————————— 27

9. A Nice Bike it is! ——————————————————————————————— 30

10. T-Rex Window ————————————————————————————————— 33

11. The Long Line ————————————————————————————————— 37

12. Assassin ——————————————————————————————————————— 39

13. Bad Dog! ——————————————————————————————————————— 42

14. The Chase ——————————————————————————————————— 46

15. The Spooky House ——————————————————————————————— 48

PART II:
Medium Takes (500-2000 WORDS)

1. Lunch Break — 54
2. Silvo — 59
3. The Train Pusher — 65
4. I Love Horse(s) — 71
5. Weather the Storm — 75
6. Texting vs. Calling — 82
7. The Long Sleep — 89
8. The Last Human Teacher — 93
9. House Husbands — 98

SUPPLEMENTS FOR EXPANSION ACTIVITIES

Supplements 1: Summaries — 104
Supplements 2: Illustrations — 109
Supplements 3: Writing — 111
Supplements 4: Media — 119
Supplements 5: Interviews — 124
Supplements 6: Language Expansion — 128

HOW TO USE THIS COLLECTION

This book is a collection of 24 open-ended stories on some creative and unexpected topics, each followed by a number of discussion activities and creative projects. One of the big challenges as an ESL teacher is to get students to *engage* with literature. That is why the stories in this collection venture a bit outside the box, with topics designed to get them thinking in new ways. The stories in this book will challenge the students' assumptions about gender roles, relationships, the meaning of success, and even reality itself. Students will be driven to engage with the stories, whether they agree or disagree with some of the views in them.

Reading truly is a two-way street. That is why this collection is focused on also involving students with the creative process. The activities and projects that follow each story are focused on getting students connecting to the stories through writing. And, as the title suggests, all the stories in this collection are left open-ended to help students engage directly with literature by writing their own ending. They will also come to understand the underlying purpose of creative writing: communication.

Each story includes a **Before You Read** section that preteaches some vocabulary and presents discussion questions to get students thinking about the topic of the story. These can be done individually, as a class, or in small groups.

The stories themselves come in two formats. Appropriately, the two levels of length and difficulty are also meant to help achieve slightly different learning goals:

The 15 **Short Takes** are under 500 words and usually one page long. They tend to be more general and universal in nature. They are also completely open-ended and meant to spark debate and discussion. Many of the extension projects following these stories are intended to help students create their own flash fiction, a popular term nowadays for fiction that is extremely short in length, typically only a few hundred words or less.

The 9 **Mid-Length Stories** are between 500 and 2000 words long and are meant to engage the students on a more literary level, giving them a bit more to sink their teeth into and generally with a more detailed plot progression. However, all stories are left open-ended to the extent that the main goal is still to engage students in their own content creation as well. As a result, they are also intended to be expanded upon.

All stories are followed by **After You Read** discussion questions that help students think more deeply about the plot and themes of the story. They also allow the student to reflect on what they liked or didn't like. Some of these questions ask about the ending of the story. Students can use this time to discuss a new ending, but be sure not to preempt any writing task in the **Projects** section. Students may want to use the discussion from **After You Read** to gather ideas before writing, however.

Finally, each story is followed by a series of creative **Projects** that ask students to engage more personally with the topic of the story. Students will find themselves writing about one particular character, or drawing a scene from the story or connecting the topic to their own lives. And as mentioned, students are always asked to write an ending to the story. Each writing assignment is designed to take about one page, but you may want to specify a longer or shorter story. You can also decide whether to assign all the projects or do just one or two. You can also do one in class and assign another one for homework or as a longer-term project.

The last part of the book consists of 17 **Supplements** to help students find additional creative outlets with the stories whether through illustration, dramatic creation, or an interview. These supplements can work with any story in the collection to extend the lesson beyond the projects in the creative Projects section.

At the end of the day, hopefully these stories will help students have fun with the process of reading and creating writing. And while this book was created with the ESL classroom in mind, the stories have been scaled appropriately to be useful in any classroom.

Taylor Sapp—2018

PART I:
Short Takes

1. Choose a Path — 2
2. Family Matters — 5
3. Lunch of the Twelve — 8
4. The Glass is Half . . . — 13
5. Pick a Pet — 17
6. Gifted — 20
7. Joe and His Beans — 24
8. The Eyes Have It — 27
9. A Nice Bike it is! — 30
10. T-Rex Window — 33
11. The Long Line — 37
12. Assassin — 39
13. Bad Dog! — 42
14. The Chase — 46
15. The Spooky House — 48

CHOOSE A PATH

Before You Read

1. If you could only choose
to be one of the following,
which would you choose?
a. rich
b. famous
c. beautiful
d. immortal (to live forever)

Write the letter of the definition next to the matching word

1. *wealth (n.)* ____
2. *casino (n.)* ____
3. *transformation (n.)* ____
4. *exquisite (adj.)* ____
5. *perfect (adj.)* ____

a. a place used for gambling, including
card games, slot machines, and other
betting games
b. extremely beautiful
c. entirely without any flaws, defects,
or shortcomings
d. a change in form, appearance, nature,
or character
e. a great amount of money, valuable
possessions, or property

CHOOSE A PATH

Four young people stood at a road that split in four directions. There was a sign pointing each way with a single word.

The first sign said, "*Wealth*." The first young person took this road and followed it to a great *casino*. Here, the first young person turned a single dollar into many millions!

The second sign said, "*Beauty*." The second young person took this road and followed it to a huge beauty salon. Inside, they went through a *transformation* and when they came out, all would say they were the most *exquisite* person in the world!

The third sign said, "Love." The third young person took this road and followed it to a small café with delicious pastries and coffee. Here, the third young person met the most wonderful partner they could ever have imagined and had two *perfect* kids and a happy family.

The fourth sign said, "?" The fourth young person took this road and followed it to …

THE END?

After You Read

1. Which path would you choose?
2. Would you be willing to take the fourth sign? Why or why not?
3. What are some meanings you can think of for the fourth sign?
4. The characters in this story have no gender. Did you imagine them as male or female? Why?

Projects

1. Continue the story! Write about a page. Here are some questions to consider as you write:
- Where does the fourth sign lead?
- What happened to the fourth person after they went there?

2. Interview 3 or more people and ask them the question from **Before You Read** above. Use the chart below. Or create your own. (See Supplement 5:1)

Afterward, compare their answers. How are they the same or different? What do you think about the results?

- 4 -

Interview Question:

If you could only choose to be one of the following, which would you choose?

a. rich   **b.** famous   **c.** beautiful   **d.** immortal

Name	Answer	Reason

FAMILY MATTERS

Before You Read

1. Which situation do you think is best for a married couple with children? Which is most similar to your family?
   a. The wife stays at home with the children while the man goes to work.
   b. The husband stays at home with the children while the wife goes to work.
   c. Both the husband and wife work while the children go to daycare or have a babysitter.

Write the letter of the definition next to the matching word

1. *head of the table (n.)* ____
2. *housewife (n.)* ____
3. *househusband (n.)* ____
4. *elaborate (adj.)* ____
5. *daycare (n.)* ____

a. supervised daytime care for preschool children
b. fancy or complicated
c. a married man who stays at home to take care of the children or home
d. a married woman who stays at home to take care of the children or home
e. the most important place at the table, at one of the short ends

FAMILY MATTERS

237 WORDS

Four families in the beautiful, quiet town of Englishville were having dinner. They were all very tired. All of their kids were thankfully playing together in the other room!

Akira and Sachie, seated at the *head of the table*, were the hosts of the dinner party. Akira had finished another long day selling Toyotas at a nearby dealership. Sachie, the *housewife*, had been cooking and cleaning all day, but was satisfied that all were enjoying her *elaborate* traditional Japanese dinner of white rice, breaded pork, and pickled vegetables.

Sarah and Sam were on the left side of the table. Sarah was exhausted from her busy day as boss of a large company. Her husband Sam was a *househusband* who was also tired from a busy day of running, playing soccer, and a little bit of video games with his three kids.

Gabriela and Juan sat on the right side of the table. They had both just gotten home from work and picked up their kids from *daycare*. They were happy to learn today that their children were a year ahead on their reading skills, thankful that the very expensive school was teaching them well. Someday Juan and Gabriela hoped to read a book with them together if they could find the time!

And sitting at the opposite end of the table was the newest family in town.

"So," Sachie began, "What can you tell us about yourselves?"

THE END?

After You Read

1. What do you think about the different families in the story?
2. Why do you think it's traditional in many cultures for husbands to work and wives to stay home?
3. What is your family like, or what do you think you will do in the future?
4. Do you think it's more difficult to go out to work,
or stay-at home with children? Why?

Projects

1. Continue the story! Write around a page. Here are some questions to consider as you write:
- Who works in the new family?
- How are the children taken care of?
- Is there anything unusual about their family situation?

2. Draw a picture of:
   a. Your family including your parents, brothers and sisters, and any pets.
   b. Your current house or childhood family home. Describe as many details as you can about it to a partner or the class.

3. Interview 3 or more people about parents. Do both parents work or does one or both stay at home? (See Supplement 5.1 for a worksheet you can use)

4. Interview 2-3 peoples about their opinion on housewives or stay-at-home dads/house husbands. (See Supplement 5.1 for a worksheet you can use)

THE LUNCH OF THE TWELVE

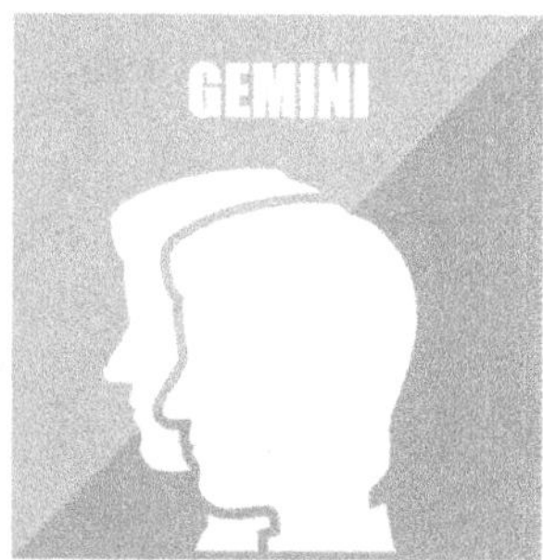

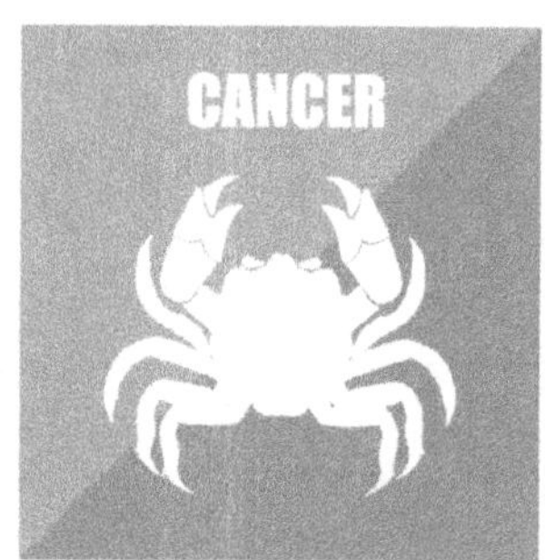

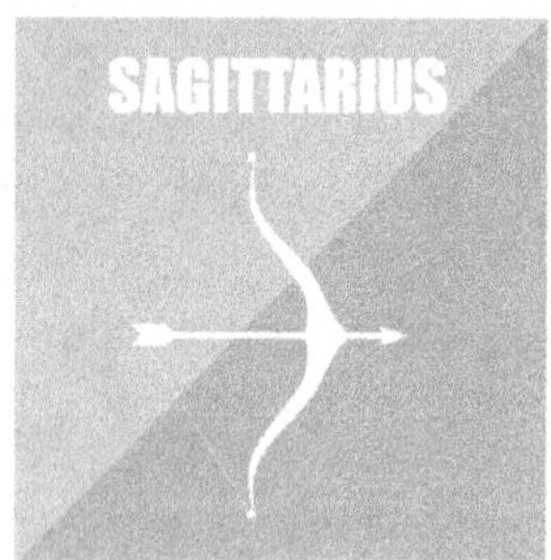

Before You Read

1. The picture above shows the names of the Western star signs, based on astrology. What do you know about star signs? Do you know any other sets of birth signs?
2. Do you know your star sign? If so, what do you know about it?

Vocabulary

Write the letter of the definition next to the matching word

1. *pound (v.)* ____
2. *frantically (adv.)* ____
3. *weep (v.)* ____
4. *font (n.)* ____
5. *MIA (n.)* ____

a. to express sadness or a powerful emotion by crying

b. stands for Missing In Action, originally used to describe soldiers who were not found after a battle, used informally to refer to someone whose whereabouts aren't known

c. the way a letter looks; a complete assortment of type of one style and size

d. to strike repeatedly with great force with a fist or something that is not sharp

e. desperately or wildly with excitement or fear

THE LUNCH OF THE TWELVE

Around a large round table at a sandwich shop sat twelve friends. They each had a menu and were trying to make a decision about their lunch. The shop had a special deal that if they all ordered the same sandwich they would all be half price! But how would they decide?

The first, Aries, boldly declared, "A grilled chicken sandwich would be the best, and I'll fight any who disagree!" *pounding* the table hard with its fist.

The second, Taurus, calmly and politely smiled. "I believe egg salad is a good choice as well." No one was going to change Taurus's mind.

The third, Gemini, was looking back and forth *frantically*. "They all sound good! I can't decide!" he said.

The fourth, Cancer, overwhelmed by conflicting emotions, started to *weep*.

The fifth, Leo, stated strongly, "We've waited far too long! I'll go to the counter and order for us all!"

The sixth, Virgo, was too busy examining the *font* on the menu and dirt on the counter to focus on the order.

The seventh, Libra, insisted on taking a vote to decide which sandwich should be ordered.

The eighth, Scorpio, smiled and pretended to agree with Libra, but was still angry from a disagreement from the previous month and planned to vote against whatever Libra decided.

The ninth, Sagittarius, was *MIA*, having gone to the restroom and gotten busy wandering around the shop.

The tenth, Capricorn, insisted on ordering the club sandwich, the best value on the menu.

The eleventh, Aquarius, wanted to suggest asking for a pizza instead.

The twelfth and last, Pisces, busy daydreaming, asked, "Where do you think the word 'sandwich' comes from?" And was planning to write a poem about it.

In the end, they ordered . . .

THE END?

After You Read

1. How would you describe the personalities of each star sign in the story?
2. Which one matches your personality?
3. Which character(s) have the best trait(s)?
4. Which have the worst traits?
5. None of the characters genders is indicated in the story. Did you assume any were male or female? Why?

Projects

1. Continue the story! Write around a page. Here are some questions to consider as you write:
- What will they order?
- Who will agree or disagree?

2. Look up your star sign on the Star Sign Personality Chart. Does the description match your personality or not? Now look up your family. Write one page on what parts of the descriptions you agree and disagree about for you and your family.

3. Use the Star Sign Interview chart below to interview your classmates/friends/family about their star signs. Share the most interesting results with the class.

ARIES: Fire
(3/21-4/19)
 	
+ Energetic, active, bold, daring
– Selfish, impulsive, violent
☺ Leo, Sagittarius
☹ Cancer, Capricorn
	TAURUS: Earth
	(4/20-5/20)
	
	+ Patient, reliable, persistent,
	  placid, honest
	– Jealous, possessive, greedy
	☺ Virgo, Capricorn
	☹Aquarius, Leo, Gemini
		GEMINI: Air
		(5/21-6/20)
		
		+ Talkative, easy-going, versatile,
		  witty, youthful, lively
		– Nervous, indecisive, cunning
		☺ Aquarius, Libra
		☹Virgo, Taurus

CANCER: Water
(6/21-7/22)
 	
+ Sensitive, protective, caring
– Moody, overemotional
☺ Scorpio, Pisces
☹ Libra, Aries
	LEO: Fire
	(7/23-8/22)
	
	+ Artistic, outgoing, aristocratic,
	  loving, generous, dignified
	– Bossy, domineering, pompous
	☺ Sagittarius, Aries
	☹Scorpio, Taurus, Aquarius
		VIRGO: Earth
		(8/23-9/22)
		
		+ Intelligent, meticulous, modest,
		  practical, diligent
		– Conservative, overcritical, fussy
		☺ Capricorn, Taurus
		☹ Sagittarius, Gemini, Pisces

LIBRA: Air
(9/23-10/22)
 	
+ Charming, romantic, sociable
– Indecisive, flirtatious, gullible
☺ Gemini, Aquarius
☹ Capricorn, Aries, Cancer
	SCORPIO: Water
	(10/23-11/21)
	
	+ Determined, courageous,
	  emotional, intuitive, intense
	– Jealous, secretive, obsessive
	☺ Pisces, Cancer
	☹ Aquarius, Leo, Taurus
		SAGITTARIUS: Fire
		(11/22-12/21)
		
		+ Honest, intellectual, jovial,
		  freedom-loving, independent
		– Restless, crude, careless
		☺ Aries, Leo
		☹ Pisces, Virgo

CAPRICORN: Earth
(12/22-1/19)
 	
+ Hard working, patient, practical,
  reserved, disciplined
– Negative, rigid, grudging
☺ Virgo, Taurus
☹ Libra, Gemini, Aries
	AQUARIUS: Air
	(1/20-2/18)
	
	+ Friendly, independent, original,
	  inventive, honest, popular
	– Contrary, unpredictable,
	  detached
	☺ Gemini, Libra
	☹ Capricorn, Taurus, Scorpio
		PISCES: Water
		(2/19-3/20)
		
		+ Compassionate, sensitive,
		  nature loving
		– Vague, escapist, too idealistic
		☺ Cancer, Scorpio
		☹ Sagittarius, Leo

Interview Questions:

> What is your star sign/Element/Personality? Do you agree/disagree with your star sign? Why do you think Star Signs are so popular?

Name	Star Sign/Birthday	Personality	Agree/Disagree?
YOU:			

Conclusions: Were any results surprising? Were any results similar to what you expected?

THE GLASS IS HALF . . .

Before You Read

1. Do you think the glass in the picture is half-full or half-empty?
2. Do you know the meaning of the expression "The glass is half-full"? What about "The glass is half-empty"?
3. Which of those two expressions best describes you?

Write the letter of the definition next to the matching word

1. *optimist (n.)* ____	**a.** extremely bad
2. *pessimist (adj.)* ____	**b.** a person who sees most things in a positive way
3. *grumble (v./n.)* ____	**c.** a person who sees most things in a negative way
4. *terrible (adj.)* ____	**d.** lucky
5. *fortuitous (adj.)* ____	**e.** to complain sullenly

THE GLASS IS HALF . . .   243 WORDS

Happy and Moody are best friends despite their differences.

Every day, like today, they both wake up at 6:00 am.

Happy always looks at the clock and says, "It's good to be up early. Now I have the full day to enjoy!"

However, in his house, Moody usually looks at his clock and *grumbles*, "I wish I could sleep longer."

After getting ready, both of them usually walk outside to meet at the nearby café.

Today it is raining, and unfortunately neither of them have umbrellas.

Happy just smiles and says, "Look, a free shower!" and pulls out a bar of soap.

Moody frowns and says to himself, "My hair will look strange and my clothes will be ruined!" He tries to cover his head with a newspaper.

Usually they meet every morning at the café around 6:30 am. But today there is a sign that reads, "Closed for Remodeling—Sorry!"

"Sorry? This is *terrible!*" Moody says, "There is nowhere to go! I might as well go home and back to sleep all day, for this is sure to be a sign of bad luck!"

"No, this is *fortuitous!*" Happy never stops smiling. "Now we have a chance to try that new café down the road!"

Moody shook his head. "No matter what, you're such an *optimist*. How annoying."

Happy just laughed. "No matter what, you're such a *pessimist*, but that's what makes you special!"

"So, what should we do next?" Moody asks.

THE END?

After You Read

1. What does Happy do that makes Moody call him an *optimist*?
2. What does Moody do that makes Happy call him a *pessimist*?
3. Which character are you more similar to, Moody or Happy? Why?
4. What are some benefits of being an *optimist*? What are some drawbacks?
5. What are some benefits of being a *pessimist*? What are some drawbacks?

Projects

1. How does their day continue? Write about a page.

2. Try to think of the best and the worst days of your life. Write 1 page about your best day. Then write 1 page about your *worst* day.

3. Try to think of a bad event that happened in your life? Was there any good side to the situation?

4. *Interview*: Ask 3-5 people about the best and the worst things that happened in the past week. Use the frame on the next page.

Interview Question:

Name	Good Thing	Bad Thing

After the interviews, look over the responses and answer the
following questions.

1. Who had the best experience this week? Why?
2. Who had the worst experience this week? Why?
3. What are some positive and negative comments you can make about each?

PICK A PET

Before You Read

1. Do you have a pet? If so, describe him/her/them? If not, would you like to have one?
2. Which type of animal would make your ideal pet? Why?
3. Which type of animal would you not like to have as a pet? Why not?
4. Look up the following animals online:
   - Siberian husky
   - python
   - Russian blue
   - Komodo dragon
   - tarantula.
5. Which do you think would make a good or bad pet? Why?

Vocabulary

Write the letter of the definition next to the matching word

1. *regret (v.)* ____	**a.** having soft, light, long hair.
2. *fluffy (adj.)* ____	**b.** smart or intelligent
3. *clever (adj.)* ____	**c.** covered with a small light layer of hair
4. *shell (n.)* ____	**d.** something living or alive
5. *live (adj.)* ____	**e.** a hard, outer covering of an animal
6. *fuzzy(adj.)* ____	**f.** to feel sorry for something you did wrong
7. *exotic (adj.)* ____	**g.** special or rare

PICK A PET

302 WORDS

Today was little Trevor's 10th birthday, and his dad had promised to take him to the local pet store to get him ANY animal he wanted! Dad was really hoping he wouldn't *regret* his promise.

As Trevor and his dad walked around the store, he couldn't believe all of the different animals that were there!

First, they looked at the dogs: big dogs such as German Shepherds and Bernese Mountain Dogs, and little dogs, like Chihuahuas and Pugs. A Siberian husky caught his eye with its wolf-like look.

But he wasn't sure if he wanted a dog, so Trevor continued to the cats. Black cats, white cats, orange, *fluffy*, hairless: he saw them all. He was especially taken with a gray-haired, blue-eyed Russian blue. It looked so *clever*!

But a cat or dog was so normal. Maybe he wanted something more *exotic*?

So he went to look at the turtles. They were cute with their *shell*, but maybe not very fun as a pet. The same went for the lizards, although the big Komodo dragon looked like a small dinosaur!

Then he saw a big snake, a really scary looking python. But it needed to eat *live* mice once a week. Trevor wasn't sure he could do that!

Next, he saw a huge tarantula. It was *fuzzy*, orange, and black. It was so scary looking and easy to take care of. Of course, his mother would never come in his room again if she saw it.

"What do you think, Trevor?" his dad asked, crossing his fingers and hoping for something easy, like a cat, small dog, or maybe a turtle.

"I'm not sure yet, Dad!" There were so many amazing pets to choose from! How to decide? Was there anything else? Trevor couldn't decide until he was finished looking. . .

THE END?

After You Read

1. Which pet from the story would you choose? Why?

2. Which pets do you think are the easiest to take care of? Which do you think is the most difficult?

3. What pets are most popular in your home country or city? What are the l east popular?

Projects

1. Continue the story! Write around a page. Here are some questions to consider as you write:

- Which pet does Trevor choose?
- What do his parents think of the pet?
- Does he have any problems with his pet?

2. Write around one page about your favorite pet you have or had. If you've never had a pet, write about a friend or family who has or had a pet you really loved or hated!

3. Create your perfect pet! Say what kind of animal it is. Describe it in detail, including its name, gender, size, what it looks like, and its personality.

Draw a picture of your pet

GIFTED

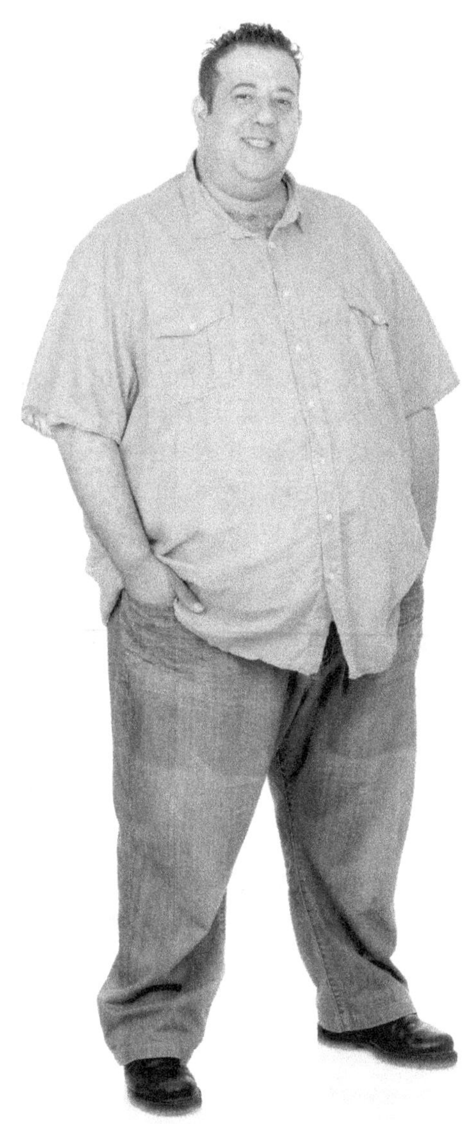

Before You Read

A *euphemism* is a mild or indirect word we use in place of a word that is more offensive or negative.

Look at the man in this picture above. We can call him fat, overweight, large, round, or big-boned. Which of those terms do you think can be offensive? Which are *euphemisms*? Why do you think we use *euphemisms*?

Vocabulary

Write the letter of the definition next to the matching word

1. *gifted (adj.)* ____
2. *special (adj.)* ____
3. *talented (adj.)* ____
4. *slow (adj.)* ____

a. having great talent or ability, sometimes used as a euphemism for having a learning disability
b. being able to do something very well
c. different from what is ordinary or usual, sometimes used as a euphemism for having a learning disability
d. lacking in perception or understanding; mentally dull

GIFTED

Mom was on the phone, shaking her head and looking very confused. I was eating pizza and drawing.

"Repeat that again. You want her to join this *gifted* club?" she said.

In the time Mom had been on the phone, I'd already been able to draw a sketch of her holding her phone close with one hand and scratching her head with the other. I was a very gifted artist.

"So, it's not about art?" Mom looked disappointed, looking out the window at November rain. "So what about . . ." She looked worried, then her sad downturned face turned to a slight smile. "Thank God, it's not about the social . . ."

She looked at me and didn't finish her sentence. She thought I didn't know what she meant. She glanced at my red knit cap sitting next to the drawing which I always wore to cover my ears when I went to school, or anywhere. It protected me from all of the loud noises and always made me feel safe!

There were a lot of things I didn't like, such as too much noise, cheese, dirty hands, small talk, anything spicy, female teachers, airplanes, animation that wasn't Disney, and certain insects, especially flies. But spiders I find kind of cute.

And so on. I knew I was a bit *special* this way. I was told this many times by everyone: by Mom and Dad; by Mr. Ross, the principal; by Sandy, my fifth-grade homeroom teacher; and by all the kids like Malik and Sally and Chaney who didn't talk to me except to make fun of me.

Special. Gifted. *Slow.*

"Ok, so hold on, when you say 'gifted' what do you mean? Like really smart or . . . you know, like not . . .?"

Mom was still struggling with her phone call. I think she was saying the same thing for ten minutes. It must have been too long because she slammed it on the table with finality.

"I give up," she said. I couldn't completely follow but I wanted to know. Being asked to join a group was exciting to me!

"So, can I join the gifted club?" I asked.

She took my right hand, as my left was busy finishing my drawing, another thing that made me special!

"Honey, I don't want to use that word anymore."

"Why not? I'm not gifted? Can I be special?"

Mom sighed again.

"You are very special to me."

I finished and showed her my drawing. She smiled so big it made me so happy to see her frustration go away.

"You are *talented*, honey, and skilled, and wonderful."

"So, do I get to join the gifted class?"

Mom thought carefully.

"Well . . ."

THE END?

After You Read

1. How is this story about euphemisms?
2. What are the different euphemisms used? What are they describing?
3. Do you agree or disagree with how they are used in this situation?
4. What other euphemisms can you think of?
5. When do you think it might be good to use euphemisms?
6. When might it be better to be direct?

Projects

1. Continue the story! Write around a page. Here are some questions to consider as you write:
- What does the mother say to her daughter at the end?
- Does the daughter join the gifted class?
- What is the class like?
- What problems does the daughter have at school?

2. Can you think of a situation where euphemisms were used? It could be a something that happened to you or to a friend or family member? Write a page about the experience.

Think of a word with a strong negative meaning such as died or dangerous. Then, try to think of a word or expression that you can use in place of the original word. For example, sometimes we say that someone passed away or is in a better place instead of saying they died.

A euphemism might sound like the original word or use more gentle language. Sometimes it might be a funny description.

Try writing an explanation or drawing a sketch to describe your euphemism.

Original Word	Euphemism
	Explanation

3. Do some research. Make a list of five or more euphemisms.

Write each euphemism and its real meaning. Had you heard any of these euphemisms on your list before? Where might you use them?

Word	Original Meaning	Euphemism Meaning

JOE AND HIS BEANS

Before You Read

1. What is a fairy tale? Can you think of any examples?

2. Do you know the story of Jack and the Beanstalk? What do you know about it or what can you guess from the image above?

Write the letter of the definition next to the matching word

1. *beans (n.)* ____
2. *plow (v.)* ____
3. *dough (n.)* ____
4. *slink (v.)* ____
5. *urge (v.)* ____
6. *gag (v.)* ____
7. *ain't (v.)* ____

a. to encourage someone to do something
b. (here) to move quickly across something
c. a slang term for money
d. to be unable to breathe because something is in your mouth
e. to move slowly and carefully from fear or shame
f. casual slang for "am not"
g. a seed from certain plants that is eaten as a vegetable

JOE AND HIS BEANS

Joe was walking home from the store one day, a long walk, when the *beans* his mother had sent him to buy slipped from his hand and into the road he was *plowing* through.

"Smart move," he was able to say aloud sarcastically, "I guess I'd better find them." One problem though—he couldn't. He thought for a second about what to do, and realizing his only option, he headed back for the store to buy some more beans.

But just as he started, he spotted an old man on the side of the road with a small stand and a sign that read "Delicious Beans for Sale."

The sight of the old man made Joe think, "Why haven't I seen this man before?" But even more, why hadn't he noticed a man selling just beans a lot closer to home than the usual store, a 7-Eleven that had great prices and delicious burritos as well.

Even though he was surprised by this mystery bean seller, Joe wasn't stupid. So he walked up to the old man and asked for some beans.

"I need five beans," Joe said, "I'll give you seventy-five cents for them." Now all he needed was burritos. The old man signaled yes, and he swapped the beans for the *dough*.

But he said something that surprised Joe, "These are no bad beans, but they *ain't* no good ones either." The old man talked funny with a weird accent. "Just remember, NEVER put them in hot water, okay?"

Joe got a little frightened. He wanted to get away from this man really quick. So he *slinked* away, and hurried home to give the beans to his mother.

Joe said, "Here, Mom, sorry I'm late. You can cook these beans, but don't use hot water, I was warned."

He thought she got the message so he went to his room and read a bit and waited.

\#

He got a nice surprise at dinner time.

The beans were just sitting in a pot of hot, boiling water. Joe almost fainted in shock! He had no idea what would happen to the beans, and he didn't want to know. His mom *urged* him to try one.

"No," Joe said, "I can't. I was told not to put them in hot water. Who knows what could happen!"

He imagined the beans growing in his stomach, coming out just like in the *Alien* movies. He could also see himself *gagging* and choking and finding out the hard way that these beans and water weren't meant for each other.

But his mother was determined, and much more stubborn, than he was.

"I will never eat those beans!" Joe said. His fight lasted five minutes, after which he was force-fed one.

As he touched the tip of his tongue . . .

THE END?

After You Read

1. What will happen to Joe? Do you think the beans are dangerous? Magical? Or just disgusting?

Most fairy tales have a message or moral. What is the message or moral of this story?

2. This story is based on a famous fairy tale called Jack and the Beanstalk. Some famous fairy tales are listed below. How many of these do you know?

3. What other fairy tales do you know? What is your favorite fairy tale?

Famous Fairy Tales

- Rumpelstiltskin by Brothers Grimm
- The Princess and the Pea by Hans Christian Andersen
- The Little Match-Seller by Hans Christian Andersen
- Hansel and Gretel by Brothers Grimm
- The Little Mermaid by Hans Christian Andersen
- The Emperor's New Suit by Hans Christian Andersen
- Little Red Riding Hood by Charles Perrault
- The Ugly Duckling by Hans Christian Andersen
- Cinderella (traditional)

Projects

1. Continue the story! Write around a page. Here are some questions to consider as you write:
- What did the beans taste like?
- What happened to Joe after he ate them?
- What happened to his mother?
- Did anything grow?

2. Choose a fairy tale from the list above, or another that you like and know well. Write a half-page summary about what happens in the story, and the message or moral of the story.

3. Create your own fairy tale. Write about one page. Be sure to include a moral or message to your story.

THE EYES HAVE IT

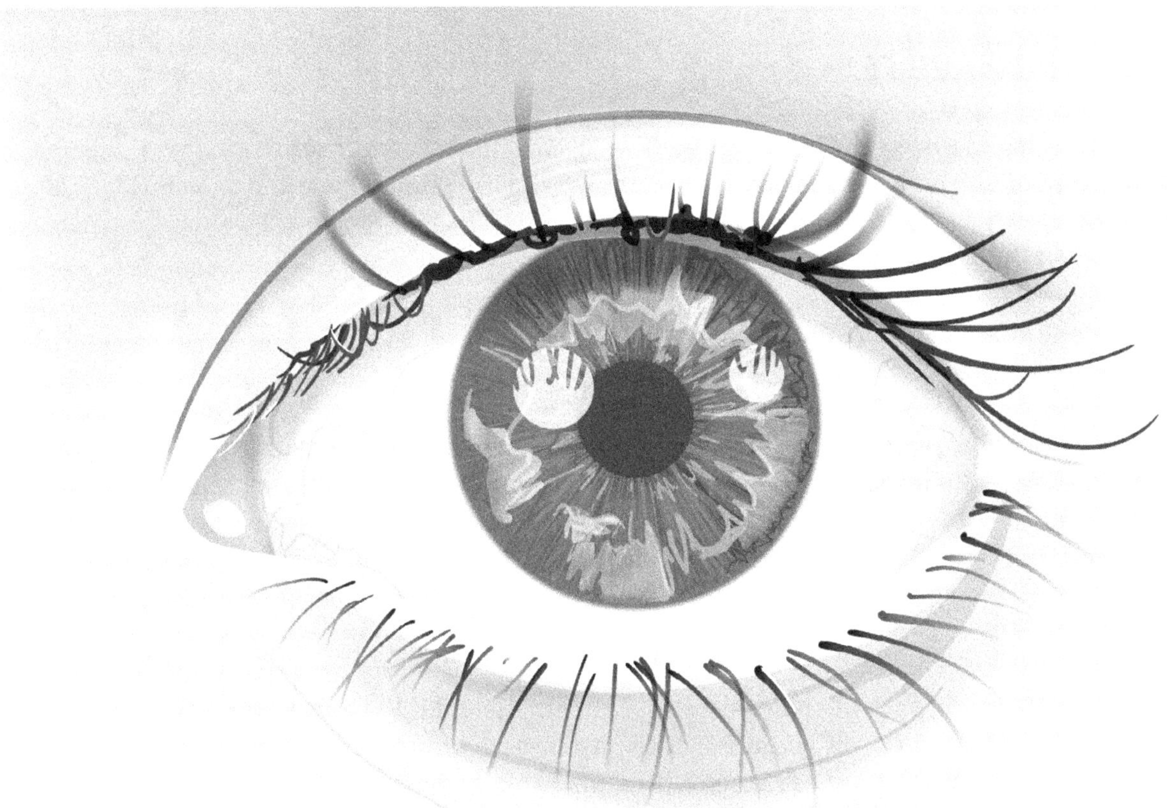

Before You Read

1. How many words can you use to describe eyes?

2. In the picture, find the pupil and the iris.

3. When does the *pupil* get bigger? When does it get smaller?

Write the letter of the definition next to the matching word

1. *dilate (v.)* ____	**a.** to become wider or larger
2. *biology (n.)* ____	**b.** the study of living organisms
3. *gorgeous (adj.)* ____	**c.** light created by the sun or nature
4. *natural light (n.)* ____	**d.** the science of life and living things
5. *biology (n.)* ____	**e.** very beautiful

THE EYES HAVE IT

296 WORDS

I was standing in line at the cafeteria, checking Facebook, Instagram, WhatsApp, Line, and five other social media apps on my phone. I wanted to see if she'd liked my posts.

So I didn't know she was standing right next to me.

"Hi," she said, as I turned and realized it was her. I jumped.

"Hi," I said, as calmly as possible.

I put my phone away, took a deep breath, and looked her in the eye, trying to remember what I'd just learned in my *biology* of human behavior class yesterday. If you want to know if a man or woman likes you, look at the pupils! Big black *pupils* means they like you—or maybe it's just really dark!

She was looking at me. I would describe her beauty, but I couldn't do it justice, so just picture the most *gorgeous* woman you know and it wouldn't even come close!!

Her eyes are brown, so it wasn't easy to spot the pupils. I didn't want her to know what I was doing, so I tried to be quick. The pupils were *dilated*! They were large, very large! Awesome! I glanced around the room. There was lots of *natural light*. Sometimes a dark room could make pupils big. But the room was light and she was looking at me, pupils almost fully dilated.

She likes me! Now I had to be strong. My plan for a while had been to invite her to watch a movie some evening. *The Goonies* was the movie that I'd overheard her talk about in our *biology* class together. She always sat with one of her girlfriends in the front. I always sat in the back.

I tried to draw the courage to speak up and I . . .

THE END?

After You Read

1. What does the main character claimed he learned about eyes from his class? Do you think this is true or not?

2. Do you think the main character of this story is right or is he making a mistake? How would you feel in this situation?

Projects

1. Continue the story! Write around a page. Here are some questions to
consider as you write:
- What did he say?
- How did she reply?
- What happens when they meet again?

2. This story is also about a possibly embarrassing romantic
misunderstanding if he's wrong.

Have you or someone you know ever been in a situation of one-sided
attraction? For example, did you like someone who didn't like you?
Or did someone like you, but you didn't like them? Write a page about
your experience!

3. Look at the next 5 people you talk to. Notice their eye pupils and the light.
Do the people you are talking to have *dilated* pupils?

A NICE BIKE IT IS!

Before You Read

1. Do you have a bicycle? How often do you ride it?
2. Have you ever had any unusual experiences riding your bicycle, such as an accident or meeting/seeing strange people?

Write the letter of the definition next to the matching word

1. *support (v.)* ____	**a.** a part of a bike or car that makes the ride feel smoother
2. *a grand (n.)* ____	**b.** \$1,000
3. *shocks (n.)* ____	**c.** food and other commodities sold by a grocer
4. *groceries (n.)* ____	**d.** to bear or hold up

A NICE BIKE IT IS!

"That's a nice bike."

"Thanks. It cost me quite a bit."

"Yeah . . . nice *shocks*, firm *support*, a narrow little racing-seat, you must be quite the rider."

"You think so? Really, I just ride on weekends. You know, back and forth from the coast. It's relaxing."

"We could use a young man like you."

"Excuse me?"

"Good riders are hard to find."

"What does that mean?"

"You even have a nice little basket."

"That's for *groceries*. Sometimes I ride to the supermarket, or the mall, or whatever."

"Yeah, maybe you could use it to carry something for us."

"Us? What are you talking about?"

"We'd pay you very well."

"Pay me well for what?"

"For working for us."

"Doing what? Not drugs, right?"

"You'd make good money."

"What, selling drugs?"

"You'd just be taking a nice ride from point A to B. That's all."

"No, no, no, no."

"The starting pay is two *grand* a trip."

"I said no!! No way. . . . wait did you say two grand?"

"That's right."

"Two grand . . . ? Whoa! I could pay off my student loans!"

"So what do you say?"

"Well . . ."

THE END?

After You Read

1. What can you guess about the two characters?

2. What do you think one wants the other to carry?

3. What would you do if you were in this situation?

4. This story is written with all dialogue. Is it easier or more difficult to read this story than a story with descriptions and other words?

Projects

1. Continue the story! Write around a page. Here are some questions to consider as you write:

- What kind of job does the main character decide to do?
- What happens next?

2. What was your most exciting/, scary, or unusual experience while talking or to a stranger? Write a page-long story about the experience!

3. Write your own dialogue scene. Write one page of talking between two characters without any description outside of the words of the characters. Use the prompts below for ideas.

Setting	Characters	Situation
at school	best friends	arguing or fighting
at Starbucks	siblings	romance
at karaoke	parent and child	an expensive new item
at a movie	teacher and student	criticizing
at the beach	coach and athlete	showing off
at a restaurant	boyfriend and girlfriend	feeling sick
shopping	strangers	in danger
having a party	staff and customer	seeing someone famous

T-REX WINDOW

Before You Read

1. Describe the T-Rex dinosaur in this picture.
2. Have you ever seen a dinosaur in a museum before? Have you ever seen one in a movie or somewhere else? Describe your experience.
3. How do you think you'd react if you saw a dinosaur in real life?

Write the letter of the definition next to the matching word

1. *extinct (adj.)* ____
2. *gasp (v.)* ____
3. *trickle (v.)* ____
4. *dismayed (v.)* ____
5. *glare (v.)* ____
6. *eternity (n.)* ____
7. *silly (adj.)* ____
8. *ridiculous (adj.)* ____
9. *imagination (n.)* ____

a. infinite time; duration without beginning or end
b. to flow or fall in small drops
c. to be worried
d. forming mental images that are not real
e. laughable
f. absurd, irrational
g. to stare angrily
h. a sudden, short intake of breath, as in shock or surprise
i. ended or died out

T-REX WINDOW

431 WORDS

Just as George was being eaten by the T-Rex, he woke up from the terrible dream.

Gasping for air, sweat *trickling* down his face, he looked around the peace and quiet of his room. It was just a bad dream!

George laughed to himself as he got out of bed slowly. It had seemed so real, like many dreams do. But he was okay. And besides, as he'd learned in school last week, dinosaurs were *extinct*.

He looked over at the clock and was *dismayed* to see he'd slept in far too long. He quickly changed his clothes and went to the bathroom to brush his teeth. He then popped open the blinds to greet the sun that poured in, and jumped back at the sound of a mighty roar.

Nose pressed to the window, an angry looking T-Rex was *glaring* at him!

Too shocked to respond, George froze. After what seemed like an *eternity*, his mom's angry voice rang from downstairs.

"Georgie! What are you doing? The school bus is here!"

George looked again at the T-Rex and smiled but was not greeted by a smile back. He raced down the stairs to find his mom holding a breakfast bar and his backpack.

"Mom, I can't go outside. There's a T-Rex out there!" he said.

His mom shook her head angrily. "I'm not in the mood today Georgie. You're going to hold up the bus again," she said.

"Mom, I'm being serious. If I go outside, the T-Rex is going to eat me!"

"Georgie, I think you should be more worried about what your mom's going to do to you if you're late to school again, instead of some *silly* dinosaur."

She had a point.

"Dinosaurs are extinct. Right, Mom?" It had to be impossible. He must have still been dreaming. Maybe he still was dreaming now. If I go outside and the T-Rex eats me, I must still be dreaming.

"All I know is, no more Jurassic Park movies for you for a while, Georgie."

George was starting to come down. It was just too *ridiculous* to imagine. They'd been talking about dinosaurs at school. He'd been watching movies, even playing a dinosaur hunter computer game. Surely it must be all his *imagination*!

George thanked his mom and kissed her, then snatched his bag and his breakfast. He put on his backpack, put on his shoes, and went outside to see the bus waiting for him down at the end of the street.

Behind him, he heard a soft, heavy breathing sound and turned to see . . .

THE END?

After You Read

1. How would you feel if you were in George's situation? Would you go outside?
2. What would you have said to your mom?
3. Have you ever had a nightmare where you saw a dinosaur or something scary? What was it?
4. What do you think happens next in the story?

Projects

1. Continue the story! Write around a page. Here are some questions to consider as you write:
- What did he see when he turned around?
- Is he still dreaming?

2. Can you remember a scary nightmare you had? Summarize it in one page.

3. Imagine an image from a scary nightmare you've had. Draw a sketch of the nightmare below.

4. Keep a dream journal. Keep this paper or a notebook near your bed and try to record at least 3 dreams.

Dream Journal

Day	Dream (Describe in a short paragraph)	Was it a good dream? Nightmare? Why?

THE LONG LINE

Before You Read

1. Have you ever waited in a long line? When was it? Where was it? What were you waiting for?
2. Have you ever gotten lost? How did it feel? How did you figure out where you were?

Write the letter of the definition next to the matching word

1. *aimlessly (adv.)* ___	**a.** covering a large distance
2. *stretched (adj.)* ___	**b.** to adjust to surroundings or situation
3. *breathtaking (adj.)* ___	**c.** amazing, fantastic, wonderful
4. *infinity (adj.)* ___	**d.** something without end
5. *reorient (v.)* ___	**e.** without a goal or purpose

THE LONG LINE

200 WORDS

Terence was busy updating his status on his phone when he noticed the line. His friend's Instagram picture of Niagara Falls was a clear view of the amazing waterfalls. He liked it, of course, and commented, "*Breathtaking!*"

He had moved on to viewing another friend's Tumblr pictures of their little baby Rory in his pumpkin baby costume when he suddenly re-entered the world by noticing that he'd been following the line for a while now to his left.

Terence stopped and looked around, trying to *reorient* himself and figure out exactly where he was. He had been wandering *aimlessly*, he realized, and didn't immediately recognize this place.

He was standing on the sidewalk on a two-lane street that changed to one-lane with cars parked solidly along both sides. To his left, a line of people extended in front of him curving to the left two blocks ahead. To his right, the line *stretched* in a straight line disappearing in the horizon.

"Where's the end of this line?" he asked, expecting an answer. But none was given.

Instead Terence found himself nervously looking back and forth at *infinity*. The best answer that he could come up with was . . .

THE END?

After You Read

1. What was Terrence doing while he was waiting in line? What are the drawbacks of using your smartphone too much in public?
2. What do you usually do while you are waiting by yourself?
3. Do you use your smartphone? What apps do you usually use?

Projects

1. Continue the story! Write around a page. Here are some questions to consider as you write:
   - What is Terrence waiting for?
   - How long does it take?
   - Does he finally get to the end of the line?

2. What was the longest line you ever waited in? What was the result? Was it worth waiting? Write 1 page about the experience.

3. Interview 5 people about the longest line they ever waited in. (See Supplement 5:1 for a model interview) Was it worth waiting for them?

ASSASSIN

Before You Read

1. What is an *assassin*? What is the purpose of their job?
2. What are some other words to describe this.
3. What are some kinds of people an assassin would kill?

Write the letter of the definition next to the matching word

1. *assassin* (n.) ____	**a.** organized crime group or member
2. *have company* (v.) ____	**b.** to have someone join you at a place or event
3. *straggler* (n.) ____	**c.** a hired killer
4. *silhouette* (n.) ____	**d.** a shadow
5. *unkempt* (adj.) ____	**e.** messy; not taken care of
6. *mafia* (n.) ____	**f.** a dark image outlined against a lighter background
7. *CEO* (n.) ____	**g.** Chief Executive Officer: The top boss at a company
	h. someone who stays at an event longer than others

ASSASSIN

394 WORDS

"Please don't kill me!" is the first thing he says as he sits down.

I must not have looked happy to *have company*.

It is just the two of us in the small hotel lounge sitting in our own dark corner, a fine whisky in front of me, an even finer cigar in my mouth. The jazz band was finishing up. I was one of the *stragglers* enjoying a late evening. I would be perfectly fine waiting for quite a while, even if there wasn't a business meeting that required my presence.

But now, interrupted, I watch the man *silhouetted* sitting across from me, waving off puffs of smoke from my cigar, as he sets a small box in front of me.

I examine the box: square, varnished oak. I press a metal latch on the front and pop it open. A quick peek: a small yellow folder, .22 caliber handgun underneath.

I don't look up as I speak. "Everything seems to be in order. I prefer using my own weapons though."

I nod and assume he will be leaving, but instead he leans forward, under the dim light overhead, exposing a sweaty brow and *unkempt* mess of short curly hair.

"This is not going to be easy. Are you sure you can do it?" he asks.

I laugh.

He continues. "I mean it! I told my boss that there wasn't a person on earth that could do this! Do you know what he said?"

I nod. "I am the only one, the best. Isn't that why you came to me? There isn't anywhere I can't go, or anyone I can't reach. The person in that folder, I can promise you that you won't need to worry about them very soon."

The man smiles nervously and *shuffles* out quickly.

I'm left alone in the bar. It had been a nice few weeks of rest during the holiday season, but now the jobs would start to pick up again.

I glance at the folder, trying to imagine who it could be. I liked to guess. A *mafia* boss? A *CEO*? A *President*? I just hoped it wasn't a woman.

As I finish my glass, the bartender about to kick me out, I decide to take a peek inside the folder. The man seemed certain this would be a difficult mission. It's time to see why.

THE END?

After You Read

1. What do you think about this profession? Why do you think it's illegal?
2. Have you ever read about someone doing this in real life?
3. How do movies portray this kind of profession?
4. What other kinds of dangerous jobs can you think of?

Projects

1. Continue the story! Write around a page. Here are some questions to consider as you write:
- Who is in the yellow folder?
- What happens when the assassin goes to kill them?

2. Make a list of all of the vocabulary that describe an assassin or professional killer. Try to use vocab from the story and others you can come up with!

3. There are lot of famous movies about professional killers or secret agents. How many examples can you think of from film or TV? Write a one-page summary one of your favorite movies or stories about this type of character.

4. Make your own spy movie or trailer (See Supplement 4:1 for directions on doing this).

5. Can you think of another dangerous job? Write a page about a dangerous job someone you know has had. Or write a fictional story about a dangerous or difficult job you know about.

BAD DOG!

Before You Read

1. Do you have a pet? Describe him/her/them. If you don't, what type of pet would you like? Why?
2. Which type of pet would you not like to have? Why not?
3. Are there any expensive things in your home? Have they ever been damaged by your family or a pet?
4. Google the following: Persian rug, Qing dynasty Vase, renaissance art. Which type of art would you most like to have in your home?

Vocabulary

Write the letter of the definition next to the matching word

1. *waddle (v.)* ____
2. *sniffles (n.)* ____
3. *gigantic (adj.)* ____
4. *poison (n.)* ____
5. *feces (v.)* ____
6. *concoction (n.)* ____
7. *waft (v.)* ____
8. *vase (n.)* ____
9. *priceless (adj.)* ____

a. deadly liquid or substance.
b. to sniff repeatedly, from holding back tears or from a cold
c. very large
d. a mixture of something
e. a container to hold flowers
f. to float or be carried through the air
g. poo, solid human or animal waste
h. to walk with short steps, swaying like a duck
i. something of extremely high value

BAD DOG! 242 WORDS

"Looks good, doesn't it?" Leonard said as he tearfully placed the bowl on the ground next to Roscoe's, his big dog's favorite spot. Roscoe *waddled* over and sniffed the food curiously.

"I just added a bit of extra spice, that's all." Leonard had trouble speaking through his *sniffles*. He had to keep staring at the *gigantic* festering collection of feces on the center of his Persian rug to keep his composure.

Leonard reached down to pat Roscoe on the head, and pushed him towards the liver and rat *poison concoction*.

"Sorry, boy, but that rug's worth $15,000, and you only cost me . . ." Leonard started to break down again. He had to focus intently on the *wafting* poop directly in front of him. "I've already given you two chances, mutt; you brought this upon yourself."

Roscoe continued to sniff at his deadly dinner without taking a bite. Leonard stood watching him for another 25 seconds before he began to get impatient.

"Fine. If you don't want to do it the easy way, we'll take a little ride somewhere. I have a better idea." Leonard went to the door and grabbed the leash. Roscoe looked up and started walking towards the door. He suddenly halted right next to Leonard's priceless *vase* from the Qing dynasty. Leonard turned around.

"What are you waiting for. Don't you want to go for a nice car ride?"

Roscoe's leg lifted. The value of the vase began to decrease.

THE END?

After You Read

1. What does the title of the story mean? Do you think Leonard or Roscoe is bad?
2. How does Leonard feel about Roscoe? How do you know?
3. What is Leonard's reason for being angry at Roscoe?
4. How do you feel about having expensive art or furniture in your house?
5. What does Roscoe do at the end of the story?

Projects

1. Continue the story! Write around a page. Here are some questions to consider as you write:

- Can Leonard stop Roscoe?
- Does Leonard succeed in getting rid of Roscoe?

2. What are some ways to "pet-proof" a house? Think of a product that might help to protect floors, vases, furniture and other things from pets. Describe your product. How would it work? How much would it cost?

You can draw a sketch below or on another piece of paper.

3. Imagine a piece of artwork you'd like to have in your own home. It could be a vase, sculpture, or any other type of art. Draw a sketch of it below. Describe the materials used. Imagine where you'd put it in your house.

THE CHASE

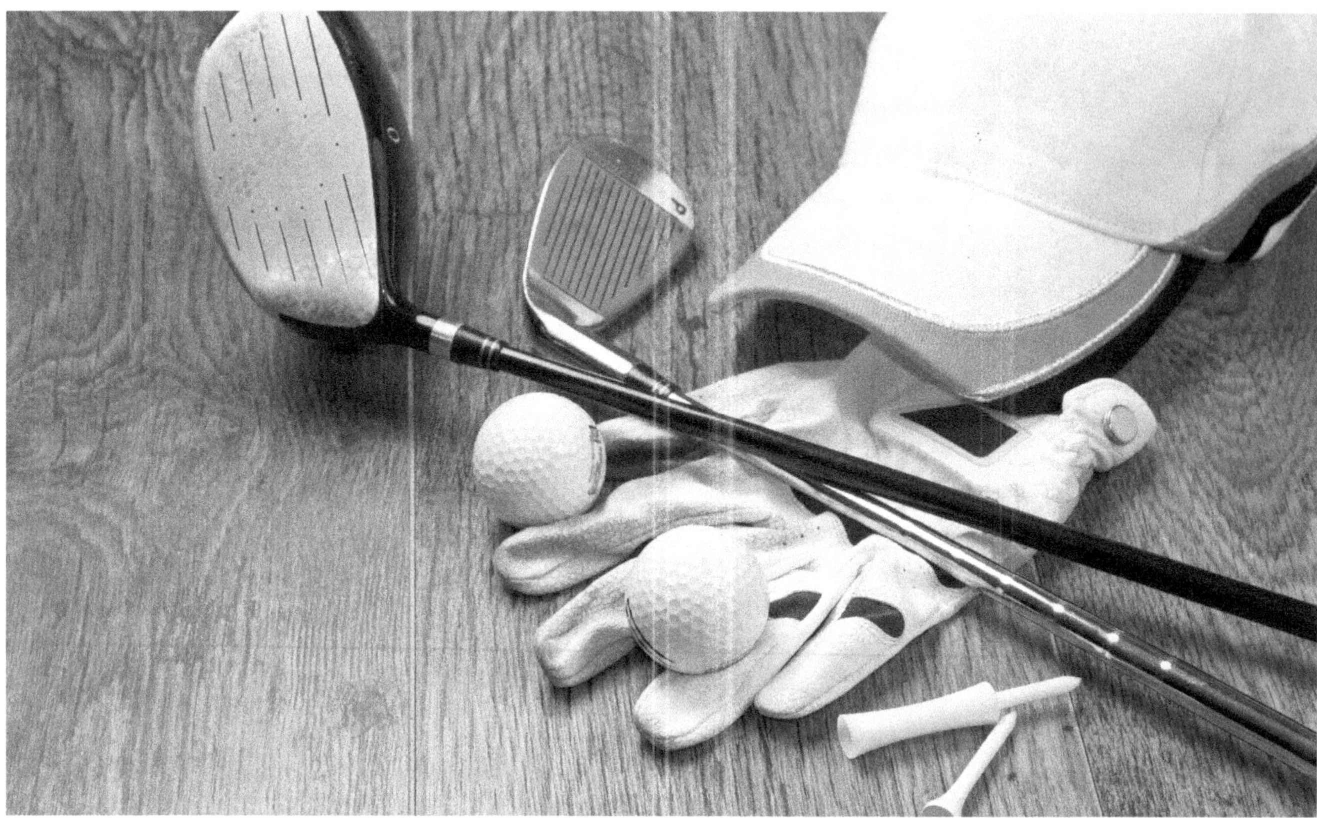

Before You Read

1. What do you see in the picture above?
2. What other golf vocabulary do you know?
3. Have you ever played golf? If yes, do you like it? If no, would you like to?

Write the letter of the definition next to the matching word

1. *hamstring (n.)* ____
2. *handicap (n.)* ____
3. *throb (v.)* ____
4. *temperament (n.)* ____
5. *limp (v.)* ____

a. to walk with a jerky movement because you are hurt
b. the tendons on the back of the knee
c. numerical measure of a golfer's playing ability, lower is better
d. pulsating or vibrating
e. emotional state

THE CHASE

As Lewis was about to attempt a sixty-seven-yard chip with his pitching wedge on the 16th hole at the beautiful Waverly Golf Course, he felt a sharp pain near his right *hamstring*. For a second, Lewis thought he'd been shot.

Then he saw a small white ball land softly a few feet away. In the distance, he could see the ball's owner, his attacker, a bald man already in flight to his golf cart.

"Where do you think you're going?" Lewis yelled. He received no response. Instead, he watched the bald man leap into his golf cart and take off. As Lewis had already been playing five strokes above his *handicap*, his *temperament* was less than stellar. This, coupled with the *throbbing* pain in his leg gave Lewis all the incentive he needed. He couldn't let this evil man get away!

Limping with all the haste that he could, Lewis slid into his golf cart and pressed the pedal to the floor. . . .

THE END?

After You Read

1. What would you do if you were playing golf and someone hit you with a ball?

2. Have you ever been involved in a chase? If so, for what reason?

Projects

1. Continue the story! Write around a page. Here are some questions to consider as you write:
- What happens in the chase?
- Does Lewis catch the man?
- What will Lewis say or do if he reaches the man?

2. What was your most difficult or dangerous moment playing a sport, such as an accident or an injury. Write a page-long story about the experience.

3. The name of this story is "The Chase." Draw a picture describing the action of this story (See Supplements 2:1 for a model).

THE SPOOKY HOUSE

Before You Read

1. Describe the house in the picture above. Have you ever seen or lived near a scary house like this before?

2. What is a *haunted* house? Do you think they are real?

3. Have you ever seen a ghost?

Write the letter of the definition next to the matching word

1. *spooky (adj.)* ____
2. *ghost (n.)* ____
3. *neglected (adj.)* ____
4. *chop (v.)* ____
5. *determined (adj.)* ____

a. not taken care of
b. the soul of a dead person visiting the living.
c. scary or related to ghosts.
d. sure, committed, settled.
e. to cut; (n.) the motion of cutting.

SPOOKY HOUSE

Tim, Parker, and Saya were walking home from school when they heard a strange sound. They all stopped to look at the source of the sound. Parker, who was new to the area, hadn't seen the house before.

"What is that?" he asked.

"I think it's that house again" Saya said nervously, pointing at it.

The house.

They were standing right next to an old *spooky* house. It looked at least a hundred years old! The house was dark gray and black and looked *neglected*, like it was falling apart. Some windows were broken, and the door was leaning sideways. The grass was long and unkempt. It did not look like an inviting place.

"Does anyone live there?" Parker asked.

Tim shook his head. "No one knows"

Saya was looking more visibly scared. "Some people say the family that used to live there was murdered and have become *ghosts*! They will attack anyone who enters."

"Ghosts? That ridiculous!" Parker said.

"Well, I heard the house is filled with deadly ninjas that will *chop* your head off if you try to enter!" Tim motioned the sword chop with his hands.

"Ninjas? No way!" Parker shook his head. "It's probably just the wind making noise in that empty old house. I'm going to look inside and settle this for sure!"

Tim grabbed his arm. "No! My dad told me dangerous criminals might be in there so we have to stay out!"

"Well, just make sure to call the police if I don't come back in 10 minutes!"

Both Tim and Saya tried to convince Parker not to go, but he seemed *determined* to prove the house wasn't so spooky after all. . . .

THE END?

After You Read

1. Why do you think Parker is willing to go in the house?
2. Why do you think Tim and Saya don't want to go in?
3. Would you go in the house? Why or why not?

Projects

1. Continue the story! Write around a page. Here are some questions to consider as you write:
- What does Parker find inside the house?
- What happens to him?

2. Create your own profile for Tim, Saya, and Parker (See Supplement 1:3 for a model). Try to imagine as many details as you can, including age, gender, nationality, hobbies, interests, and so on. age/gender/nationality/hobbies and interests.

3. Draw a picture of the Spooky House. Try to imagine it from the story.

PART II:
Medium Takes

1. **Lunch Break** ——————————————————— 54
2. **Silvo** ——————————————————————— 59
3. **The Train Pusher** ——————————————— 65
4. **I Love Horse(s)** ———————————————— 71
5. **Weather the Storm** —————————————— 75
6. **Texting vs. Calling** ——————————————— 82
7. **The Long Sleep** ————————————————— 89
8. **The Last Human Teacher** ——————————— 93
9. **House Husbands** ——————————————— 98

LUNCH BREAK

Before You Read

1. What does *teleportation* mean?
2. What examples of teleportation can you think of in TV, film, or other media?
3. If you could use a teleportation machine, where would you go for lunch today? For dinner? On vacation? For study or work?

Vocabulary

Write the letter of the definition next to the matching word

1. *sheepishly (adv.)* ____
2. *acclimate (v.)* ____
3. *tolerant (adj.)* ____
4. *commotion (n.)* ____
5. *retort (v.)* ____
6. *frightening (adj.)* ____
7. *instantaneous (adj.)* ____
8. *calibrate (v.)* ____
9. *barren (adj.)* ____

a. to reply to in a sharp way
b. accepting of things different from what you are used to
c. unproductive, empty
d. scary
e. occurring instantly
f. to determine or measure something effectively
g. violent, confusing motion
h. in an embarrassed way because you did something wrong
i. to adapt to a new environment

LUNCH BREAK

"Hajime Mashide."

Tom raised an eyebrow at his son's guest, who had just spoken.

"He said 'Nice to meet you.'" Chester smiled *sheepishly*.

His son had just blinked in from Tokyo where he was studying Japanese at Meiji University, so it was to be expected for Chester to need a moment to *acclimate*. Chester's guest, Masahiro, a PhD student, apparently didn't speak any English. What else was new? But nonetheless, Masahiro was already enjoying some wine.

BZZZT

Tom heard the familiar sound as Janice appeared on the teleporter dressed in the traditional garb of some African nation where she was serving in the Peace Corps, fixing houses and whatnot.

Tom had made his own lunch-blink to their home in Fresno, California from his corporate accounting position in Dover, Delaware not long ago. The morning's drama in the office had included a broken water pipe in the bathroom. Tragically, neither of the sinks were working and Tom had had to use Purell hand sanitizer all morning, which he wasn't a big fan of as it was supposed to dry out the skin.

"What's for lunch, Dad?" Janice asked.

"You can ask Mom as soon as she arrives." Tom looked at his watch. Usually Donna had everything laid out in advance."

"By the way," Janice spoke hesitantly as she took a seat to the left of her dad at the head of their rectangular table, "A friend of mine should be blinking in any second." The way she said 'friend' had just a little too much emphasis for Tom's liking.

Tom shook his head. "I wish you'd told us before so your mom could have gotten extra." Unless it's anything too spicy, he thought. Unfortunately, the rest of the family had a much more *tolerant* palate than he did.

As if on cue, Donna appeared, her two Lululemon totes filled with whatever mysterious lunch she'd decided to bag today.

"So what is it today, Mom?" asked Janice.

"Thai curry," she began as the kids cheered and Tom dropped his head. "Sort of. It's actually from Myanmar. Supposedly, theirs is a lot less spicy." She met the glimmer of hope in Tom's eyes, a communication that said "Trust me," though he was skeptical.

As she began setting the food on the table Janice had already popped in and out with another place setting. Donna met her husband's worried glance again. "Don't worry. There's lots extra. Who's coming? Is it Parker again?"

"No, her name is N'Gogo. . . ." Janice answered.

"That's interesting. Is her family from Africa?"

"Yes. And so is she."

"She's working with you?"

"Yes. We're building a house."

"She doesn't have one?"

"Dad! She's never lived in a real house before. Right now, we're building the first house out of stone she's ever lived in. She's used to mud and twigs."

And with that, N'Gogo blinked in looking around the room in amazement. She had short hair, a nose ring, and was clothed in a dirty brown shirt and shorts. She started to sit on the floor near the dog's bowl until Janice collected her and brought her to the table.

Tom glared at his daughter angrily.

#

In the kitchen, Tom was having it out with his daughter.

"You're kidding, right?" Tom pointed to the table, where she was using the spoon to drink from her water glass, and Instagramming the food on an iPhone at least two model years old.

"So just because she's poor and can't read, she's an animal to you?"

"Has she been inoculated . . . with anything? Or fumigated?"

Janice shook her head

Tom continued. "When she sees our house and goes back to her little village, do you still think she's going to be happy with her simple stone house? When she sees your brother Chester's smart clothes, and the hologram 3D on the wall, what's she going to think?"

"Dad, you know that will never happen! She will be happy as long as she has food and a house!"

"I'm sorry, honey. I should at least thank you for not bringing a boy."

Janice *retorted* with a *frightening* laugh.

Janice smiled darkly. "I don't think you'll have to worry about that." She flashed an odd-looking black ring and stormed out of the kitchen. Tom heard a brief *commotion* as his daughter apologized and grabbed her guest.

When he'd re-entered the room, thankfully they'd both blinked out, having taken their lunch to go (with the plates).

Tom sat down with his wife, Chester, and Masahiro to hopefully have a peaceful lunch.

But it was not to be.

#

"But Dad, I want to see other worlds!" Chester was arguing again about the study abroad program on Mars. Thankfully Masahiro had finished, bowed deeply in respect, and blinked back to his afternoon classes. Donna had smartly blinked back to work as well.

Tom laughed. "What for? You could spend every evening or weekend at a different place on Earth and still not get everywhere, and you want to waste your time on *barren* chunks of rock? None of the other worlds offer anything that our great planet doesn't!"

Interplanetary blinks were unfortunately not *instantaneous*. Secretly, Tom was happy that Mars was only an 8-hour blink away, compared to somewhere like Titan or Prollux that was days or even weeks.

Chester didn't give up. "And how do you know that? Aren't you the one that says you can't truly judge a place until you've been there?"

"But what happens if you meet a girl, one of those green ones . . ."

"A Sh'ga. So what if I did?"

"Don't be absurd, their language hasn't been *calibrated*, how would you talk to her, or her family?" He tried to imagine a nice family Christmas or Thanksgiving with the in-laws.

His son gave up and blinked back to his classes. Tom would sign up his son for the program later as a surprise. He looked forward to Chester's excited response.

"Just stay away from any green girls," he would tell him.

As Tom ate his lunch alone, it did occur to him that he should at least be thankful his daughter was dating someone from Earth . . .

THE END?

After You Read

1. How is the word *blink* used in this story? Why do you think this word is used?

2. Do you think teleportation technology will be possible in the future? Why or why not?

3. In this story, the daughter brings home a woman from a different race. Do you agree or disagree with her dad's reaction? Why?

4. How would your parents react in this situation?

5. Have you or anyone you know had this type of situation before?

Projects

1. Continue the story! Write around a page. Here are some questions to consider as you write:

- Will the dad accept his daughter's new girlfriend?
- Follow one character. What do they do for the rest of the day? Where do they go for dinner?

2. Where would you go if you had a teleportation machine? Write a one-page story about where you would go for one day!

Draw a sketch of the story **(see Supplement 2:1)**.

Design your own teleportation machine! Make sure to give it a name and a few special features!

SILVO

Before You Read

1. Do you remember your first day of elementary school? How was it?

2. What about your first day of high school or university or language school?

3. Did you ever change schools? Was it difficult to make the change?

4. How can a new student make friends?

Vocabulary

Write the letter of the definition next to the matching word

1. *eyepatch (n.)* ____
2. *skull and crossbones (n.)* ____

3. *principal (n.)* ____
4. *occupied (v.)* ____
5. *pretend (v.)* ____
6. *stale (adj.)* ____
7. *acknowledge (v.)* ____
8. *bonkers (adj.)* ____
9. *excused (adj.)* ____
10. *one-on-one (adj.)* ____

a. a symbol of pirates, or poison. It looks like a head with two bones crossed beneath it
b. see, recognize
c. slang for crazy
d. a face-to-face encounter
e. allowed to leave
f. the head of a school
g. a small piece of cloth worn over one eye
h. used by someone or something
i. old, rotten
j. to act as if something is true when it is not real, to make believe

SILVO

"Don't be afraid," the teacher said.

Charlie stood at the door, the entrance to his new classroom at his new middle school, in a new town, looking at new faces and a new teacher. And they were all staring at him.

"Class, this is Charles Richmond. He will be joining our class from today. Please make him feel welcome."

"Hi Charlie," the class said in unison.

"Hi," Charlie replied as strongly as he could.

The teacher smiled sweetly, but also condescendingly. Her name was Miss Markham, or so he had been told by the *principal*, who had led him here and left him in his new environment.

"Charlie, you may take the open seat in the back."

Charlie looked around the room casually, trying to stay cool. There were five rows of desks, each row *occupied* by two students, except for two seats in the back.

Charlie slowly walked down the rows to an empty seat next to a dark-haired boy wearing an orange shirt. Charlie could see the boy was talking to him, but too softly to hear.

"What did you say?" Charlie said as he sat. The boy surprised him by letting out a scream.

"You are sitting on Silvo!" he yelled.

Charlie jumped up in shock. There was no one there! He looked around, all eyes on him.

"Charlie, the seat on the corner," Miss Markham was pointing.

Charlie saw the empty seat in the row behind him and moved towards it slowly, watching the girl sitting next to him. She was shaking her head. He found himself saying, "Sorry," but he wasn't sure why.

Charlie looked over at the kid in orange. He was talking softly to the space next to him, his hand patting the air.

"Class, shall we continue with our reports?" the teacher asked. She looked around. "Which group would like to present next?"

The boy in orange was waving his hand frantically. "Steve and Silvo."

Steve jumped up and ran to the front of the class. He stood in the front of the class with a poster in his hand. He was waving towards the aisle.

"Come on, Silvo." He looked at Miss Markham. "He always gets shy in front of the class."

Miss Markham smiled, "There's nothing to worry about Silvo. Everyone is very interested to hear your report, aren't they?"

"Come on, Silvo!" The class chanted in unison.

Steve smiled. "Oh, now he's coming! You ready to give our report, Silvo?"

Charlie was confused, he whispered to the girl next to him, "Who is Silvo?"

"His friend," she replied.

"But there's no one there!" Charlie said.

The girl opened her mouth, but didn't say anything else.

Charlie listened as Steve gave his report on the state of New Jersey.

Half the time, he would say nothing and look at the space next to him, watching 'Silvo' speak. After the report was finished, Miss Markham asked, "Questions?"

A couple of students raised their hands and asked Charlie a few questions.

"Questions for Silvo?" Miss Markham asked.

A boy wearing an *eyepatch* with a *skull and crossbones* raised his hands.

"Which one of you worked harder on the report?" The kid was smirking.

"Silvo and I always share the work fifty-fifty." Steve said.

Charlie raised his hand.

"Yes, Charlie?" Miss Markham asked.

"I'm sorry, but I don't understand." Charlie said.

"About New Jersey?" Steve replied.

"No. Why are you all *pretending* about this 'Silvo?' Are you all trying to play a joke on me?" He was sure that must be it.

"Miss Markham, what is he talking about?" Steve was looking at the teacher.

The girl sitting next to Charlie elbowed him. The rest of the class was staring.

Charlie had never really liked being the butt of a joke, and he had also never been shy to assert himself. If they were playing a joke on him, he wasn't going to go along with it.

"Well, I'm not going to pretend. I mean, what kind of name is Silvo, anyway?"

The kids around him were telling him to shut up.

Miss Markham pointed at him. "Charlie, please go to the principal's office, right now," she said.

"What? But . . ."

"Not another word."

Charlie stood up and walked out. As he left he could hear the teacher's words behind.

"It's ok, Silvo. The new student was just making a joke."

#

Charlie sat in the principal's office, which smelled *stale* of old paper. The principal looked bored.

"You weren't listening to me before, were you?"

Charlie didn't want to answer.

"Steve Renfield has some . . . issues he needs to get over, and we have all agreed to help. Steve has a little imaginary friend named Silvo, and it's important that we all *acknowledge* him."

"That's *bonkers*! He's not real."

"Are you sure about that? Just because you can't *see* him, that doesn't make him less real to Steve. Well, for now he needs to believe he's real. Without Silvo, he won't even come to school. Your whole class is trying to help Steve, and you need to help too."

#

By the time Charlie was *excused* from the principal's office, it was lunchtime. When he got to the cafeteria, he saw Steve sitting alone with a tray in front of him, and another next to him.

Charlie walked up. Steve was again in the middle of talking to Silvo. When he looked up, he started to shake.

"Hey, it's okay!" Charlie said.

"You're the new kid that hates Silvo. Well, he doesn't like you either."

Charlie sat down across from Steve.

"I don't hate Silvo."

"You don't?"

"No, I really don't. I'm sorry I was a bit nervous. It is my first day, after all. Hey Steve, who do you and Silvo usually hang out with?"

"Well, usually Silvo and I are too busy to hang out with anyone else."

"Really? Well I don't know anyone else here yet, so I was thinking maybe we could hang out after school."

Steve looked shocked. "Really? You want to hang out with us?"

"Sure. What do you guys like to do?"

Steve looked at Silvo. *"Well we often shoot baskets after school. There's a hoop at my house."*

"Cool, I play basketball too! Maybe we can play some one-on-one?"

"You mean one-on-one-on-one?"

"Sure." Charlie thought, glad to have a friend.

Or two.

THE END?

After You Read

1. How does Charlie feel at his new school? Are the other children welcoming to him?

2. Who is Silvo? What do we know about him?

3. How was the class treating Steve and Silvo? Would you do the same?

4. What is an imaginary friend? Did you have one when you were little?

Projects

1. Continue the story! Write around a page about another new student joining the class the next day.
- How do they react to Silvo?
- What does Charlie do?

2. Going to a new school can be a very stressful experience. Imagine a new student is joining your class from today. What are some things you could do to make them feel welcome?

3. Create your own imaginary friend! Draw their picture and write as much as you can to describe them, including their name, gender, age, appearance, and personality.

THE TRAIN PUSHER

Before You Read

1. What is happening in this picture? Do you know where it was taken?
2. Have you ever been to Japan? If so, how was it? If not, would you like to go? Why?
3. Have you ever had to ride a busy train or subway?
4. Are you *claustrophobic* (scared of being in tight places)?

Write the letter of the definition next to the matching word

1. *shuffling (adj.)* ____	**a.** polite behavior
2. *contort (v.)* ____	**b.** to twist or bend
3. *meek (adj.)* ____	**c.** self-controlled state of mind
4. *stocky (adj.)* ____	**d.** to force from behind, push
5. *shove (v.)* ____	**e.** a type of Asian dumpling
6. *culmination (n.)* ____	**f.** the final result or end of something
7. *miserable (adj.)* ____	**g.** unhappy, uneasy, or uncomfortable
8. *composure (n.)* ____	**h.** having a solid and sturdy body
9. *incident (n.)* ____	**i.** gentle, not aggressive
10. *courtesy (n.)* ____	**j.** an individual event
11. *gyoza (n.)* ____	**k.** moving by sliding your feet

THE TRAIN PUSHER

1700 WORDS

Every day there were so many people. It might have been overwhelming if it wasn't my job. From 5:59 am until 8:59 am, it was my responsibility to help maintain order and balance at Saginuma Station on the Den-En-Toshi Line. The lines of commuters *shuffling* to their jobs, conforming to deadlines, *contorting* into a variety of shapes could not fit onto the train without my help. That was my job: people arrangement. It was similar to bagging groceries in that it involved careful placement and strategic thinking. And it also took a lot of strength.

My station was in the heart of Tokyo, directly in front of the downward escalator that most liked to use. Today was especially busy, as it was a rainy day. Rain meant more people would elect to take the train instead of driving. Long lines got longer. Carried umbrellas added extra bulk to fill up the precious space.

One station to my right was Rintaro, my best friend since before I could remember. Truly. Our mothers were in the hospital together. Our parents' friendship was surpassed only by our own. Once, the great Yuri, one of the few brave female pushers, had been my other support, making the perfect team. Her replacement to my left was a new staff-in-training, Shota. To say he was disappointing me would be an understatement. His *meek* manner and feeble appearance would have led me to believe he was a woman if I didn't already know this job required the services of a male.

Rintaro, by contrast, was quite *stocky*. Judo experience had given him a strong build and muscles, along with *gyoza* (permanently damaged and folded) ears, and standing nearly 185 cm he towered over most of those he pushed. I would be seen as more average, standing 175 cm with a slightly muscular build. I trained hard however, doing at least one hundred push-ups and sit-ups every morning. Along with my experience, I never felt I was deficient in the strength needed for my job, and if a situation occurred, Rintaro always came to my aid before I could even think to ask.

But today, with the unreliable Shota nearby and the rain pouring down, I felt stress. The time was only 6:20 am and things were still relatively peaceful. The time before the 6:46 am Semi-Express train was what was called Light Pushing Stage. From 6:46 am until the peak at 7:52 am was the Heavy *Shoving* Stage, followed by the lighter but still vigorous Medium Shoving Stage until the daily *culmination* of our shift following the 8:59 am local train.

During the Light Pushing Stage, the most important aspect was giving bags adequate clearance. Commuters often carried large briefcases, purses, even suitcases or musical instruments. The clearance between these bags and the doors offered us the most challenge.

But my biggest test always came at precisely 7:41 am. Or perhaps I should say she came. Of course, I didn't know her name, but I knew her as my White Beauty. She always wore a crème-colored pantsuit, pink earphones, and a matching pink iPod dangling out of her breast pocket. Her skin tone was milky white, likely of Akita heritage, and her profile was petite and curvy. It went without saying that she was beautiful. But it was more than that. There was an atmosphere, the space around her, something about her that filled the space, made even the air around her seem warm and full, especially on *miserable* days like today. My White Beauty. I dreamed every night of the day she would actually make eye contact with me.

Every morning, she would slowly appear in the back of the line at my position. I never saw her coming. Perhaps I was too busy, but I imagined her as an angel. She was suddenly just there and her milky white skin brightened my day. But as her train arrived, the long line of waiting passengers quickly overfilled the train, so I readied myself. As I began my pushing, targeting those that looked willing, or the other frequent riders I had established some sort of communion with, she always gave the slightest, most casual, yet friendly, smile that I had ever seen.

Or maybe I had seen it before, back in Saitama, in the face of my dear mother, when I would come home from school, feeling tired, saying, "Tadaima! [I'm home]" and there the smile would be. That smile I had only seen on two lovely faces before. This same feeling returned to me every morning and it refreshed me every time. It was something that I looked forward to, and something that energized me for the rest of my day afterwards.

Except for today. The 7:41 am train left and then the 7:43 am was there. I looked around curiously. Where was she? I felt lost, adrift. But there was nothing I could do.

"I need help!" Shota's crying had missed me completely and Rintaro was already running to help him. I looked and saw Shota desperately trying to shove a kimono-clad sumo wrestler onto the train. Usually such people have the sense to avoid the busiest times.

"I got it! Watch my line, Tadashi!" Rintaro said.

He charged forward, head tucked like a bull and in a swift motion slammed the sumo onto the train. The doors began to close but didn't make it all the way. Something was blocking them.

I looked over wearily at Rintaro's line; a woman's umbrella was hanging out. Still feeling a bit in a daze, I moved to her and snatched it from her hand. As the doors closed again, I flung it over her head into the train where it disappeared into the crowd. As the train pulled away the reality of what I had just done hit me with an intense force. I didn't need Rintaro's gaping expression to tell me. An important code had been broken.

 I was losing my *composure*. One might say Shota was throwing me off with his incompetence, but I had dealt with similar new staff before. I couldn't help but wonder what had happened to my White Beauty. Maybe something terrible. Or maybe just a simple cold. But even that I could barely imagine. I had never even seen her wear a facemask. She was too perfect, too much of an angel.

The next train arrived and Shota looked around desperately, perhaps planning an escape. I came over to help him without thinking. As the next group tried to pack in and the feeble Shota pushed desperately, I found my Lateral Smash to be oddly lacking strength. Usually I had no trouble pushing an extra 10-20 people onto a seemingly full-train. But with five on and others shoving from outside desperately, I felt no give. I was pressing against a brick wall. Rintaro appeared again to give the necessary final shove and as the 8:01 am train pulled away, he looked at me worriedly.

"Are you feeling alright, brother?"

I nodded, but he could tell something was wrong. I wanted to tell him the truth, but such a confession would be out of the question. They say the distance between even the closest people is infinite and there was no way I could share my secret feelings. Even with my best friend in the world.

"Shota, you can rest. We are past the most difficult part."

His eyes widened. Not wanting to risk his window, he disappeared in a flash. It was the first time I had seen him move quickly. At that moment, I really missed Yuri even more.

"You cover Shota's line. I will handle the other two," Rintaro said.

Even with my pride, I didn't want to argue, as I was barely sure I could even handle the single line by myself. So I just nodded.

The next several trains went by without serious *incident*. It took all I had to push each group on. Though I usually felt vigorous and energetic as I neared the end, I now felt so drained I could only anticipate a long nap after I finished. Hopefully I would see my White Beauty in my dreams.

The final train of the day, the 8:59 am, arrived. Seven people stood in my line as it approached. Only seven more. I looked at my regular line, where Rintaro was standing, and nearly shook from disbelief. There she was, dressed as usual, as radiant as always: my White Beauty! I looked at her for a moment but she was looking away from me. For a moment my heart leapt and my energy started to return. Then the realization hit me: She isn't mine today; I have given her to Rintaro. Friend or not, the thought confused and enraged me so much that I had to turn my attention back to my line. I thought for a moment that I could race back to my line, but such a move was more gallant than I could ever hope to be.

Instead I just counted. It would be easier to forget than to acknowledge that it would be Rintaro, not me, pushing her today. How would she handle it? It was Rintaro that was usually renowned for his gentle touch, a 'gentle giant' while I knew my style to be colder and more professional. How would she respond to his warmth? Could I lose her forever? Would I always lack the strength without her?

I put my focus into counting as I pushed all seven onto my train. . . . or were there eight? I looked up; a last-minute arrival was . . . her! For a second, she looked at me, really looked at me! Her eyes wide, deep, and filled with kindness. I was still reeling when, amazingly, she spoke!

"I am sorry to be late. See you tomorrow."

I pushed her on, trying not to treat her differently than the others as professional *courtesy*, but I couldn't help being a little bit delicate. I didn't see it but I could imagine she felt it and smiled.

And then the doors closed and she was gone. But only until tomorrow. . . .

THE END?

After You Read

1. Who is the White Beauty? Why do you think the main character is so interested in her? Why does the main character give her that name?
2. Who was Yuri? Why do you think she left? What do you think the challenges are of being a female train pusher?
3. What is a train pusher? Do you think the main character of the story likes this job? Why or why not?
4. Would you like to be a train pusher? Why or why not?

Projects

1. Continue the story! Write around a page. Here are some questions to consider as you write:
- What happens the next day?
- Will the girl come back?
- Will she speak to him?

2. Think of all the places that you have traveled by train before. Make a journal of those experiences. What was your best train ride? How about your worst? How was the train? How did the people act?

3. Imagine yourself on a packed train like the story. How does it feel? How do you react to the train pusher? Write a page-long story about it. Then, draw a picture of yourself in this situation to show your feelings.

I LOVE HORSE(S)

Before You Read

1. Have you ever ridden a horse? If so, how was it? If not, would you like to?

2. In some countries, it is usual to eat horse? Have you ever eaten horse?

3. What animals are *taboo (forbidden)* to be eaten in your country?

Write the letter of the definition next to the matching word

1. *imply(v.)* ____
2. *struggle (v.)* ____
3. *plural (adj.)* ____
4. *stand-alone (adj.)* ____
5. *sightseeing (n./adj.)* ____
6. *jug (n.)* ____
7. *determined (adj.)* ____
8. *restless(adj.)* ____
9. *culture shock(n.)* ____
10. *misunderstanding (v.)* ____

a. greater than one
b. to have trouble with
c. a large container or bottle
d. visiting places of interest
e. to fail to understand correctly
f. unable to relax, worried
g. confusion for someone who is suddenly exposed to a new culture
h. committed
i. by itself, self-contained
j. suggest without saying directly

I LOVE HORSE(S)

"We will miss you, Rachel!" My family was crying, and so was I. It was our last dinner together; after six wonderful months, it wasn't going to be easy leaving them.

I use the term "family," but that *implies* the wrong thing. Hiroko, Masaya, Satomi, and Toshikazu are only my host family. But since the day I arrived here in Kyoto, Japan six months ago, they've insisted on treating me like one of their real children.

"Special present, love horse, ne?" said Masaya. How right she was. I was looking forward to seeing my horse, Moncha, terribly, but I would miss my new family too!

Those six months, they've passed so fast!

#

Six months ago, Ma and Pa at the Sea-Tac airport, tearing up then, just as I was now. Then I was on the plane, my first time out of the US. It was the longest flight of my life away from my parents.

And Moncha.

Moncha is my Peruvian paso. I've had him since we were both seven. The hardest thing about studying in Japan, other than living with a different family and *culture shock*, was being separate from him. Until now, I had never gone more than two days without a ride.

My dream has always been to ride, breed, and take care of horses. I was lucky enough to grow up on a farm where that was possible, and even luckier to get my own horse. I realize that sounds pretty crazy to some people who think a horse is something only rich kids have. In fact, my family here in Japan never seemed to quite get it. They seem to *struggle* with the *plurals* here. "Horse," they would always say, and I would correct them: "horses."

#

The time I spent in Kyoto, studying at university, the kind Sato family . . . My first night. I was so confused by the little things. Like when I emptied the bath after finishing, they asked me why I had done that.

"I take bath too," Toshikazu had said. But surely, he didn't want to use the same water?

But he did. The whole family did! The Japanese bathroom had both a bathtub and a *stand-alone* shower unit in one small room. Families would usually rinse first in the shower, and then share the same bath! Luckily, they always let me go first, because as much as I liked them, I don't think I'd want to share bathwater with even my real family!

#

They took me *sightseeing* to so many beautiful places such as Kinkakuji, the golden castle. And the Kiyomizu Shrine, where you could fill up a bottle of water for free at the huge natural spring. It was quite a sight to see the people with huge *jugs* filling up, for themselves or to sell it, even my family didn't know.

\#

I would miss Satomi, the same age as me and also in her second year in university. She was always doing her best to bring out the woman in me, a female side that I knew must be somewhere. The amount of makeup she wore shocked me, but it never looked overdone. Thanks to her she showed me how to make myself super pretty, not that it matters much for a farm girl.

\#

And Toshikazu, my host brother who was two years older. He was searching for a job while holding onto his last days of college, and *determined* to show me as much fun as possible. Even though I don't like drinking alcohol, I'll never forget the parties he set up for me and the other American friends I made at the izakayas, Japanese bar-restaurants. There were long nights singing karaoke, where I always felt they did so, so well! I became convinced our American approach to karaoke was more often than not all about volume, while Toshikazu would attack something like The Beatles' "Yesterday" with such sobriety and determination, I really felt like I was at a concert!

\#

But for all these passing memories, it is still Moncha that lingers in my mind. He must be getting *restless*.

"When he misses you he always eats too much," my mom kept saying on the phone. Well, if you've been getting fat, Moncha, I'm sure we will work it off soon!

\#

So now here I am, with my family at a huge goodbye feast with so many foods I've never tried, fish, rich meats, and some things that scare me a bit, but I'm willing to try.

"We know you love horse," my host father says, and they are all smiling. "Present."

I look around, but I don't see anything. So I take another bite of the rich Kalbi beef. But something about the rich taste, the look on their faces makes me stop and think.

"You love horse, ne?" They are saying "horse," not "horses," and I realize something that I pray couldn't be true.

"Horse?" And I burst into tears. My family joins in, crying even more and gathering to embrace me, *misunderstanding* my emotions, which are now fully mixed.

"Horses. I love horses. Not horse!" I sob.

THE END?

After You Read

1. Think about the title of the story again. Does it have more than one meaning?

2. This story is an example of a misunderstanding between cultures. Why do you think this misunderstanding happens? What do you think you would have done in this situation?

3. Can you think of unusual foods you've eaten?

Projects

1. Continue the story! Write around a page. Here are some questions to consider as you write:

- What will she say to her family?
- How will they react?

2. What's the weirdest thing or funniest misunderstanding that happened to you here in the US? It could be a strange food, tables manners, or any cultural difference. How did you figure it out?

3. Imagine you are trying to make a poster for visitors to your country or city. What cultural values would you warn them about? **(See Supplement 2:1)**

4. There are a lot of non-English words in this story. Make a list and try to guess their meanings in English. Make a list of their meanings in your language too and share with the class!

5. Make a list of 3 or more interesting words your language and their meanings in English to share with the class.

Meaning in Your Language	Meaning in English

WEATHER THE STORM

Before You Read

1. What kind of weather do you like the most?

2. What is your favorite season?

3. Have you ever experienced a natural disaster? If so, describe the experience.

4. What is the weather like in your hometown?

5. Are any types of natural disasters are common in your hometown?

Write the letter of the definition next to the matching word

1. *Celsius (n.)* ____
2. *Fahrenheit (n.)* ____
3. *claustrophobic (adj.)* ____
4. *milquetoast (n.)* ____
5. *latitude (n.)* ____
6. *longitude (n.)* ____
7. *demeanor (n.) v* ____
8. *residential (n.)* ____
9. *acre (n.)* ____

a. the distance north or south from the equator of a point on the earth's surface

b. distance of a point on the earth's surface east or west from the prime meridian

c. a temperature in which 0° represents the ice point and 100° the steam point. Symbol: C

d. a temperature in which 32° represents the ice point and 212° the steam point. Symbol: F

e. conduct or behavior

f. an area with private houses or apartments

g. a common measure of area in the U.S. and U.K. 1 acre equals 4,840 square yards (4,047 square meters)

h. a very timid person

i. the fear of being in tight or narrow places

WEATHER THE STORM

1,523 WORDS

WEATHER CONTROL: 1/21 Sunny, 72 degrees *Fahrenheit/32 Celsius.*

The beautiful blue sky, crystal clear ocean, and white sandy beach beckoned. It was a vivid enough screensaver to look almost real. A lot better than a stuffy office.

There wasn't much you could do eighty-four stories underground. No amount of fans or air conditioning could simulate a nice natural breeze. In office G305, Brett Zoeller, a Senior Vice-President of Weather Control management, felt *claustrophobic* as usual, seated at his desk. He looked at his Omega watch. It was 10:32 am, two hours until lunch.

The requests were piled high on his desk: A couple sunny days here, a couple sunny days there. Everyone always wanted to make sure everything would be super for their party, picnic, or wedding.

Beneath the stack of endless tedium was one interesting request.

"Jennifer!" He buzzed his secretary through the phone.

"Yes, Mr. Zoeller?" she replied.

"Do you know why this Z102 was put on my desk?"

There was a pause before she answered. "I think it was delivered by a member of Mr. Carson's staff."

"Bill . . ." Brett sat back in his desk. William Carson was Chief of Management, a man who was supposed to have the final say on the big decisions, but too much of a *milquetoast* to actually make any of them. So instead of their usual typical request nonsense, all the big, important government requests were spread out and about to VPs and other lower-relegated staff.

Bill Carson was nothing more than a politician, a fool who went in front of the cameras standing next to the President, the two of them reading from their teleprompters, while the real work was done by people like Brett.

And Brett welcomed the challenge. He knew he was being watched—no, groomed—for a promotion. He had to be careful, because if he made a bad call on the important things he would also get all of the blame.

His intercom buzzed.

"Mr. Zoeller?" Jennifer asked.

"What?" He snapped, out of his daydream.

"Someone is here to see you."

"Who? I'm busy. Can you reschedule?"

"It's a rain request, sir. I think it's pretty urgent."

Brett sighed and rolled his eyes. "Fine. Give me a minute before you send him in."

Rain requests were the worst. Usually it was either religious or cultist fools with some spiritual BS or worse, a farmer crying about his poor crops, ignorant about the provisions.

He took the moment to quickly glance at the file that had caught his eye before. The header jumped out at him: Storm Request. The region was in South America, but the country was not identified, just the location by *latitude* and *longitude*, as if that was enough to keep it a secret. He could look it up in a minute on his computer.

He thought for a minute, struggling to remember the news. Wasn't there a coup or a war somewhere in South America? Chile? Guatemala? He couldn't remember, but he knew the way these things usually went. A "natural" disaster was going to be on its way to some misbehaving little locality, courtesy of Weather Control, who, of course, officially, didn't have the ability to cause "weather changes of any great magnitude."

There was a knock on the door.

"Come in," Brett said.

He slammed the file shut, grabbed one of the anonymous requests, and opened it on top of the other files with the denial stamp positioned in the air in his right hand.

The door opened, a flash of blonde, his secretary, cute, but better in her natural brunette, so he could never convince her.

"Mr. Zoeller, this gentleman is here to see you about a rain request."

A man, or rather, a walking cliché, entered. Wearing a cowboy hat, overalls, and a red t-shirt, the man had the looks of a classic farmer. His face was a mess of gray hair and a thick beard. He had a sunburned face offsetting his blue eyes that shone through. A real worker of the lands.

"Would you like to sit down, sir?" Mr. Zoeller asked.

The farmer shook his head.

"That's cool," Brett thought. Don't get too many visiting very often. He wanted to ask if the farmer was for real, or worked at an amusement park. He had seen his share of farmers in his job, pleading for their poor crops, but not one quite this crusty—as if he'd walked out of another century or the Midwest.

The farmer walked over to Brett's desk and placed a manila envelope, covered in dirt stains, in front of him. Brett took it and opened it.

"Application for rain extension?" he asked, wondering who had done the filing, and doubting whether the man in front of him could actually read.

The farmer nodded.

Brett flipped through the file. "Three denials? I think maybe you should try a church instead?" The joke lingered in the air uncomfortably. "Do you think this meeting can really make a difference?"

The farmer shrugged his shoulder.

"Well, it might." Brett leaned back, spun around in his chair and grabbed a Cuban cigar. He lit it and put it in his mouth. He offered one to the farmer, who again shook his head. Brett noticed a pipe around the farmer's neck.

Brett pointed, "You want a light for that?"

The farmer looked at him for a moment, then leaned forward. Brett flicked his gold-plated Bulgari lighter open as the farmer puffed on his pipe. Brett flicked the lighter closed and flipped it around in his hands.

"Like it?" he asked. "A present from my ex. Witch that she is, she always gave good presents. My favorite necktie was from her, too." He pointed at his plain blue and white striped tie. "It's not this one."

The farmer gave a slight nod, but no smile, no expression of anything. Was he amused by Brett's *demeanor* or offended? The man's stoicism was beginning to rub Brett the wrong way.

"You do realize, sir . . . What's your name, by the way?"

The farmer looked at the file sitting on Brett's desk. Brett glanced at the name written on the front page: Farmer.

"Farmer? Is that your first name or last name?"

The farmer nodded.

"First name?"

The farmer nodded.

"Then what's your last name?"

He looked again at the application. Farmer was written twice, in the spaces for first and last names.

"Farmer is your last name too?"

The farmer nodded again.

Well at least that's easy to remember, he thought.

"So, are you going to tell me why you want a rain extension, or am I going to have to read the file to found out?"

Brett knew the answer before he finished the question, as the farmer just kept staring, impassive. His arms were now folded at his chest, perhaps to indicate . . . Brett couldn't be sure.

So he took a look at the file. The extension was asking for 14 days.

"14 days of rain! Where?" He looked. "Palisades Farms! That's not farmland anymore. That's a *residential* community."

Or at least it was now. Brett remembered that the area was famous for its posh versions of "farmers" with their ponies or llamas for their kids. But before that, it had actually been a farm. However, all the farmers had long since sold.

"You're still farming that land? You didn't sell?"

The farmer nodded.

"How many *acres*?" He checked the file. 200 acres!

"Ok, I am beginning to see the issue here. I believe your district has already reached the legal minimum days of rain, which is eleven for the year, interspersed between September and April. But it's nothing to worry about."

The farmer produced a photograph from a bulging pocket in his overalls. The photo was of a line of dried, withered crops of . . . something.

"Is that corn?"

The farmer shook his head.

"Well, whatever it is, it doesn't look good."

The farmer nodded.

"So you need fourteen days of rain, in a row, for your crops?"

The farmer nodded.

It was all coming together. This stoic old farmer was still clinging on to 200 acres in one of the richest boroughs in the country. This was the kind of place with enough influence and money that rain was never needed. Sprinklers and immigrant hydration teams could cover any potential issues due to lack of irrigation.

But somehow this stoic old farmer was still toiling away.

"Let's see if I have this all figured out. You're clinging to the old family farm while some evil corporation wants you to sell out. Well, guess what? You should listen to them. You can sell the farm or wait until it dries out and is worth nothing."

The farmer sat motionlessly, looking down. When he finally looked up, tears welled in his eyes. He delivered a long, murderous stare, and then got up and left.

Britt sighed in relief.

"I don't make the rules. I just enforce them." he said aloud to the benefactors that must be listening.

THE END?

After You Read

1. What do you think will happen next for the farmer and his family?
2. What would you have done if you were in this situation?
- Brett
- The farmer
3. Do you think we may be able to control the weather in the future? Why/Why not?
4. How would you feel if we could control the weather? How would we decide when to have rain? Snow?
5. If we could control the weather, should we still have natural disasters? Why/why not?

Projects

1. Write a new ending for the story. Write around a page. Here are some ideas:
- Brett decides to help the farmer.
- Someone else comes to ask Brett for help.
- What does the farmer do?
- Your own idea!

2. Compare the weather in your home city to another city in another country. You may need to do some research. Fill in the Weather Information Chart below for both cities.

3. Now imagine you could control the weather for your hometown! Fill in the last column of the chart below.

Weather Information Chart

Weather Patterns:	Your Hometown:	Another City:	Your Perfect Weather:
Days of Sun			
Days of Rain			
Days of Snow			
Average Temperature			
Types of Natural Disasters			
Other Weather Patterns			

Reflection Questions

1. What are the biggest similarities between the three cities above?
2. What are the biggest differences?

DYSLEXIA

Before You Read

1. Do you find it easier to talk to people face-to-face, on the phone, or through texting or chat? Why?
   a. What is a *phobia*? Do you have any phobias? Do you know anyone with an unusual phobia?
2. SAD, or Social Anxiety Disorder, is a type of *social phobia*. What do you think that means?

Write the letter of the definition next to the matching word

1. *dyslexia (n.)* ____
2. *in-ear monitors (n.)* ____
3. *session (v.)* ____
4. *bite the bullet (n.)* ____
5. *dabble (v.)* ____
6. *ubiquitous (adj.)* ____
7. *dreadful (adj.)* ____
8. *objective (adj.)* ____
9. *stick-in-the-mud (n.)* ____

a. to do something for a long period of time
b. a learning disorder which causes difficulty reading and writing
c. extremely bad, unpleasant, or ugly
d. a conservative person who lacks imagination and doesn't enjoy doing new things
e. based on facts
f. existing or being everywhere
g. to force oneself to perform a painful, difficult task or to endure an unpleasant situation
h. earbuds, earphones
i. to try or do something occasionally

DYSLEXIA

The phone buzzed but Joe refused to answer it, or even check, because he knew who was calling. His parents were the only ones who continually insisted on calling, even though texting was so much easier.

"Sorry. Can't make it today" would read his text, just as always. It would then be followed by their call, in which he'd be asked to justify his decision. That was the way he felt, at least. Joe had a busy afternoon planned in his apartment *sessioning* Call of Duty with some friends who were scattered around the world, and he wasn't feeling his parent's Lawn Party or whatever it was they were having.

"But, come on," his mom would insist, "Andrea will be there"

Andrea was a girl he didn't like, that he hoped didn't like him either. Yet, for some reason, both sets of their parents continually wanted to match them together. It was reason enough to avoid the Lawn Party, except he knew the odds were on Andrea ditching it too, for similar reasons.

Joe's days were so elegantly devised that his quality *in-ear monitors* might as well have been glued on. They were a barrier that could remain on from his commute on the train or bus, into work, straight into his desk, and remain in his ears at his computer for a satisfying day of human-less IT work. On the off chance the earphones had to come off for a mind-numbing meeting, they remained dangling off his ears, desperate to return and protect him from the world.

Joe's life was perfect. He had everything: A modest but adequate apartment, all the tech he needed, a busy life working at an online programming job he enjoyed, and time at night to either game or *dabble* in music creation.

But of course, his parents were relentless. Occasionally he had to *bite the bullet* and endure an update on their dull lives, usually trips to somewhere sunny with lots of golf for dad like Palm Springs and sentences that began with, "Remember . . .?" followed by a name he either didn't know or didn't care about. Inevitably, they'd ask how he was doing. His response was the *ubiquitous* "Fine." His parents followed that with, "Met any nice girls yet?" That was his cue to say he was busy and get off the line.

\#

So he continued to ignore his phone and focus on his game, when suddenly he was interrupted by a knock at the door. He jumped up quickly. He was expecting a package, a new MIDI keyboard, after which it would be time to sell the old one on Craigslist.

But to his surprise, he found his father at the door. The gray-bearded figure was wearing a tan sport coat, blue pants, and a white shirt. He said something that was drowned out by a protective layer of "Tom Sawyer" by Rush on his earphones.

"Um . . ." Joe began, not sure what to say, as he popped out his support devices, keeping them closely cropped behind his ears.

"I came to pick you up for the Lawn Party," his father said. Those last two words were emphasized in an almost-sinister manner.

Oh, crap, he thought. He froze for a moment before regaining his composure.

"Yeah as much as I love a good Lawn Party. . . . actually I'm busy. I have to . . ." He trailed off, not having any particularly good ideas, but hoping that would be enough.

His father shook his head gravely, indicating it wouldn't be. "Let me make it simple. Your mother has asked me to get you, and I'm in agreement with her. Just a few hours and then you can return to what you're doing. Don't forget . . ."

He didn't say it, but Joe knew what his dad was thinking. Those stupid college loans. It was a lot of money and his father had so kindly offered to pay what was remaining, which was most of it, as an ongoing Christmas present since the previous year. Unfortunately, Joe had learned this was a Devil's Bargain. It wasn't the first time it had been used as an excuse to get him to do something, but it was getting close to the last in Joe's mind.

But today? As much as he wanted to say no, the truth was, he was just making it financially and not having to deal with fifty grand of extra debt was an absolute lifesaver. Plus, he knew exactly what his mom was thinking, and on some level, he did want to make her happy. He was their only child after all.

So, soon, after a few minutes give or take to "get presentable," as his father requested, he was sitting in a Lexus SUV, silently on his way to the Lawn Party.

"I'm glad you're coming. You won't believe what your mother made."

"Oh really?" he said with mock interest.

"Yes," his father said, coldly aware.

"I don't see the point, really. Andrea's not going to be there, so Mom is making a fuss for nothing."

His father laughed at that, in a way that disturbed Joe. He would soon see why.

#

Enjoying his mom's lemon-blueberry muffins and finding, with great difficulty, the bright side of the *dreadful* Lawn Party, Joe nodded as an old couple that he distantly remembered from his youth rattled on about their two kids that were off doing great work somewhere in the world, doing Peace Corps or Green Peace or Peace something. Some such nonsense.

He had already spotted Andrea when he came in, sitting with her parents at one of the many tables arranged on their expansive two-acre lawn, which he thankfully no longer had to mow. They were at one corner, so Joe hugged the opposite and endured as much weak conversation as possible. To his mind, anything was better than feeling pressured to talk to a girl he didn't much care for.

Andrea and her parents were neighbors, a few houses down. They had a big place with horses that no one ever seemed to ride. The single memory he had of Andrea's father was the repeated chestnut of the horses being "overpriced pets."

Joe and Andrea had supposedly, allegedly, been quite close in their very early days of youth, which Joe could barely remember. After that, they had barely spoken throughout their years in school, though their parents too often seemed to want to get together, which involved them conveniently being brought to the same places, without any real conversation ever being made. For some reason, this only seemed to convince both parents what a good match they were.

Joe supposed on an *objective* scale that Andrea might be attractive. She was in the average, or slightly above-average range, like himself. She wasn't unattractive. But she had two huge negatives: thick, blue-rimmed, 'quirky' glasses, and long, dark hair. He hated the nerdy look and he had an obsession with blondes.

Plus, with what little glimpses of her personality he got, she came off as way too much of a *stick-in-the-mud*. And he'd rather be alone than have to put up with someone else's neuroses.

Anyways, the Lawn Party had been proceeding in appropriately boring fashion when it took a dive for the worse. He spotted Andrea's parents pointing in his direction and gathering what looked like a mirror of gloom to head in their direction. As his instinct to run kicked in, his wily mother suddenly appeared from nowhere and put a hand on her shoulder.

"Oh, look who's here," her mother said, oh so cheerfully, the malice so well hidden.

Encouraged by his survival thus far, Joe deftly tuned out the greetings from Andrea's parents, only nodding at them, and then in the direction of his would-be match.

He let his mind drift out of necessity, knowing that if he could just keep his body present but mind absent, this period of nonsense would end and he could get back to missed Achievements on Call of Duty, or perhaps write a nice moody melody with his new keyboard to encapsulate the annoyance he was feeling.

But his ever-crafty mom had put two plates of food down at the table, and before he could resist, he found himself sitting, one-on-one in front of her, mining him by shaking her head with the same indignation. And with that both sets of parents disappeared and the two were left far too stranded in a sea of white chairs and tablecloths, with paper plates of smoked chicken, scalloped potatoes, and something colorfully mysterious his mother had made.

The two ate silently for some time before Andrea shockingly cut the air. "I was sure you wouldn't come."

Joe nodded. "I thought the same about you."

They continued eating. This time Joe found himself interrupting the silence for some unknown reason.

"Do your parents make you do this kind of thing often?" he asked.

"Thankfully, no, despite how much I love Lawn Parties" she answered.

"I have a good job," he said.

"Me too."

"And lots of friends."

"Me too," she repeated and he wondered if she was lying too.

She spoke softly. "Mom's always saying I need a man to be happy. Or to take care of. Or take of me, whatever that all means."

"Same thing, except for me she means a woman, of course." He had thought before of telling his parents he was gay, just as a joke, but his mom was just old-fashioned enough to freak out too much to make the joke funny. "Even if you're not my type," he added.

"Wow, I feel exactly the same way about you." She looked at him and smiled, for the first time that he could remember.

"Too much of a nerd?" he asked.

"Well, you're not bad looking. I mean clearly you don't work out, but you're not fat or ugly or anything."

They had enough in common to speak lightly enough for several more minutes before the weather took a dark turn and spelt a premature end to the party. For better or worse, they exchanged business cards before they parted.

His mother seemed both pleased and disappointed, but Joe carefully assuaged her that the two had gotten along fine, giving his dad the appropriate look to convince the both of them to press no further.

That day sowed the seeds of a friendship that led to Joe picking up the phone and answering it the next weekend. A ten-minute conversation followed about nothing (mostly a shared hatred of meetings at work), but it made his placid mood even better. So the next weekend, he made the call, and that was the beginning of something. . . . maybe not romance, but for Joe, a decent friendship was more than enough.

THE END?

After You Read

1. Dyslexia is defined as "difficulty in learning to read or interpret words, letters, and other symbols, but that do not affect general intelligence." How does it relate to the meaning of the story?
2. Do you think Joe and Andrea will become close friends or boyfriend and girlfriend? Why?
3. Do you think they're a good match? Why or why not?
4. The parents and son have a disagreement about texting vs. calling. Which do you think is more useful? Why?
5. Do you ever have issues using texting with your parents or family?
6. Who in your family prefers calling? Who prefers texting?

Projects

1. Imagine that the two main characters went on a first date. Where would they go? What would they do? Write a short story (about one page long) about the date.

2. Think of a recent interesting communication you had, and write a page-long story about the experience.

3. Make a Social Interaction journal. For the next 3 days, keep track of all the friends you talk to and how you talk to them. Is it face-to-face, on the phone, by texting or through online/social media? Write about your results. Is there any difference between online and face-to-face interaction for you?

Social Interaction Journal

Day	Text	Phone	Other (SM)	Face-to-Face
Day 1				
Day 2				
Day 3				

Reflection Questions:

1. What interesting results do you notice?

2. Is there anything you'd like to change about how you communicate?

THE LONG SLEEP

Before You Read

1. What's the longest amount of time you've ever slept?
2. What's the strangest place you've slept?
3. The picture above is an example of a bear *hibernating*. What is unusual about the way bears sleep?
4. Are there any ways to make humans sleep longer?

Vocabulary

Write the letter of the definition next to the matching word

1. *cryogenic (n.)* ____
2. *quackery (adj.)* ____
3. *diagnosis (n)* ____
4. *incurable (adj.)* ____
5. *jovial (adj.)* ____

a. good-humored
b. relating to medical cures that don't really work.
c. not curable
d. the reason for an illness or health problem
e. of or relating to very low temperatures

THE LONG SLEEP

797 WORDS

It had been a nasty disease, so rare that it hadn't had a name, much less a cure. Their doctor had inappropriately joked that, on the plus side, when you get a disease this rare and deadly, you can get it named after you!

In earlier days of human life, they would have thanked the doctor, had a good cry, and prepared for the end. The doctor had given her six to nine months, so they would have made the best of them and that would have been it. Nicole, his wife, so brave and strong, would have probably pushed him to find someone else to take care of him, as considerate and kind as she was. But Martin would have been able to say no, his best skill in their relationship. For Nicole, everything was always possible. According to her, people were divided into two categories, the "Why?" people and the "Why not?" people. She was a "Why not?" person.

He'd been afraid to even try a beer before Nicole, as the consequences of being drunk and losing control were frightening. But ever the sunshine to his raincloud, she made the absurd suggestion to "lock him up like the wolfman so he couldn't destroy the town" before trying a single Corona. Her absurdity helped Martin begin to see life differently. Though opening up wasn't easy for him, every day they were together seemed liked moving forward, capped by their honeymoon, scuba diving in the Maldives. Not only had he not even known where that was when she suggested, he'd never even left the US before that.

But their honeymoon had been the beginning of something new, for both of him. And as much as Martin questioned why his new wife would choose him, he already knew. Nicole was such a free spirit with too many stories about excess and sad memories of her kindness being abused that they definitely balanced each other out. But while their honeymoon had been the start of a new chapter of their life, it turned out to be a far different one than expected.

Shortly after the extensive testing and terribly negative *diagnosis*, Martin trembled with the fear that everything that had transformed his life would soon be taken away. Though she was the sick one, he was predictably more upset.

Until they had gotten a call from another specialist. His name was Dr. Luther Warner, and he said he was pioneering a new treatment that could lead to a cure for many currently *incurable* diseases like Nicole's. Though suspicious, the two went out to see him, and there was no way they could have been prepared for what he was going to suggest.

#

"*Cryogenic*? Freezing, like in a sci-fi movie?" Martin shook his head with disbelief.

The doctor, his bearded, *jovial* Santa-Claus-like appearance making his propositions sound too near to *quackery*, merely laughed. "This is no joke. And not only has this technology been fully tested, it has been used successfully for a number of years. However due to the cost and logistics, it is necessary for it to remain, under wraps. To put it another way, if this technology were somehow widely adopted, it could become a logistical nightmare. That's why, due to Nicole's age and extremely rare affliction, we are offering to provide her this treatment at fully subsidized cost in the interest of science and humanity."

Nicole was nodding. Martin looked at her, shaking his head. She was probably thinking it sounded cool or something.

"Honey," he said, "This is crazy. I can't believe such a thing is possible."

"I don't care," she replied, "If it could work, I'm going to try it. Besides, if I sleep long enough, maybe when I wake up they'll finally have an iPhone with a battery that lasts me more than a day!"

Martin looked at the doctor. "What about me? I have to just wait? Months, years?"

"If I had to guess, fifty to one hundred years would be a very rough estimate, based on our current research on similar neurological disorders."

Fifty years! Martin almost screamed. As the two of them were just shy of 30, he could be old enough to be her grandfather when she woke up. Worse, he'd have to live his entire life without her.

"That's why," the doctor continued, "we're going to offer you the same treatment as well."

Nicole embraced and kissed him on the cheek. "Talk about the ultimate adventure. And we can take it together!"

"Nicole, even if this works and we sleep fifty years or whatever, how can we possibly adjust to that?"

"Martin, it's your choice, and I want us to be together, but I'm not ready to die yet. . . . So will you do this?"

THE END?

After You Read

1. Do you think a 'long sleep' will be possible in the future?

2. What are some ways this could be good or bad?

3. Would you agree to a 'long sleep'?

Projects

1. Continue the story! Write around a page. Here are some questions to consider as you write:

- What does Martin decide?
- If he says no, how does he live without Nicole? How does she feel when she wakes up in the future?
- If he says yes what happens when they both wake up in the future?

2. Imagine Nicole and Martin both decide to be frozen and wake up one hundred years from now. What do you think will be different? Use the chart below to organize your thoughts.

3. Try drawing a picture of your future!

The World in 100 Years			
	Technology	People	Other
Similar			
Different			

THE LAST HUMAN TEACHER

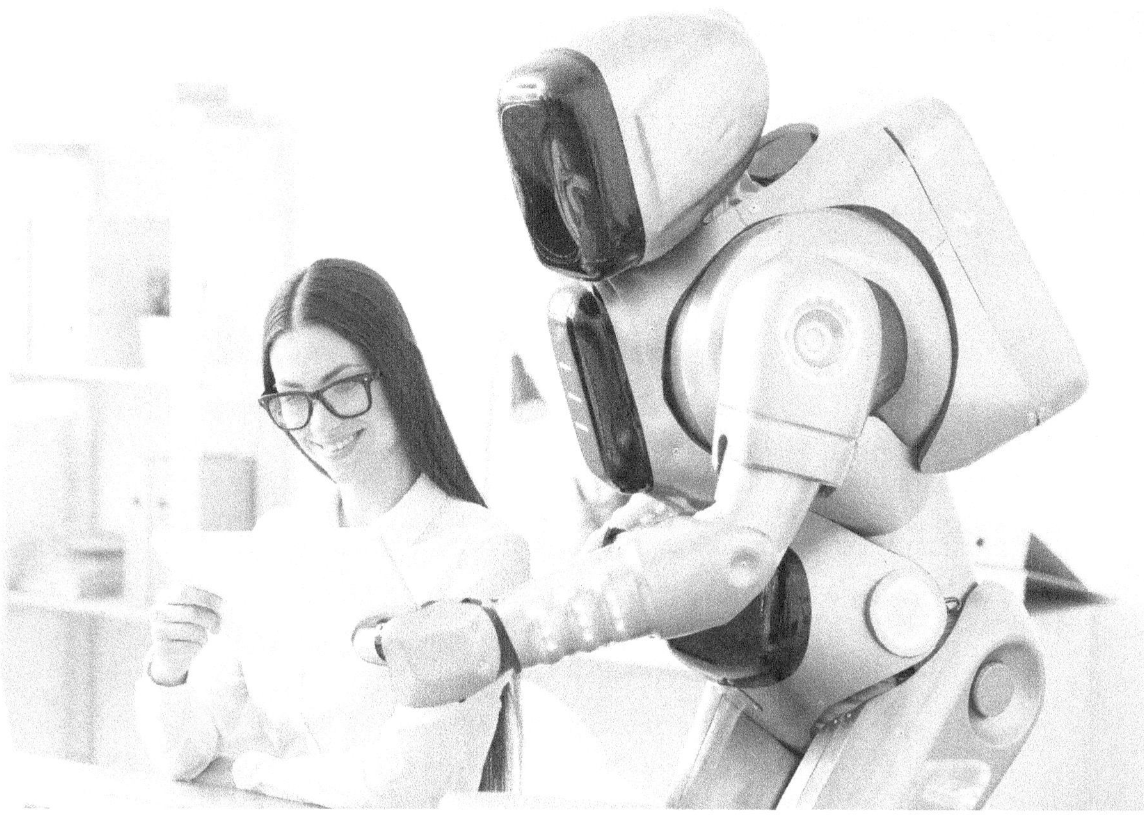

Before You Read

1. What kinds of jobs can robots do now?
2. What kind of jobs do you think robots will do in the future?

Write the letter of the definition next to the matching word

1. *simulation (n.)* ____
2. *robot (n.)* ____
3. *biometrics (n.)* ____
4. *volatility (n.)* ____
5. *contempt (n.)* ____
6. *Stone Age (n.)* ____

a. disdain, scorn
b. a machine that resembles a human and does routine tasks on command
c. something that appears to be something it is not
d. (idiom) a long time ago
e. measurements of a person's physical state or behavior
f. the tendency to turn dangerous, even violent

THE LAST HUMAN TEACHER

1,368 WORDS

At his insistence, Thurman's retirement party was a quiet drink at a local pub, just between the two of us.

"It's going to be weird being the only one left."

"No kidding. That's why I was hoping we would be having our retirement drinks together."

#

So here I sit in the "teacher's lounge." Will it have any reason to exist once I'm gone? My first day without Thurman was quiet. Now I was the last human teacher at Sherman High School, and possibly the last one on Earth! I had never been one for small talk with the *Simulations*, the *robot* teachers. The problem wasn't that they didn't look real. They were meant to look and act just like us. But there were little things. In fact, I was the only one that needed a teacher's lounge. I was the only one who drank coffee or needed to correct any work on a computer terminal, as they could all do it automatically.

There were four terminals in our room, three more than would ever be used. It hadn't seemed odd when Thurman was still there. Having extras was useful in case of tech difficulties, But the extra ones stood out that much more now, so many more than I needed.

The coffee maker, television, refrigerator: I was the only one that still had a use for any of these.

J12 and S23 sat on the couch, smiling pleasantly. They didn't seem to be watching me, or doing much of anything. They looked like us, talked like us, but every time I went in the teachers' lounge and saw them sitting, silently, because they had nothing to do or say, it really creeped me out. I knew the only reason my coworkers came here was primarily for my benefit, to foster the appearance of harmony, but it just made me feel worse: their pretending to be human. As if I could complain to T109, our principal. He was as sympathetic as I had seen, for a Simulation. I think he sat in his office silent, frozen, all day, waiting for complaints.

As for the students, they didn't seem to care about my misgivings. In fact, they thought having a real person teach them was funny, especially when I got sick. The fact that I wanted to do this was becoming more and more a point of contention. Complaints from parents were getting very close to making the school enforce the retirement that I refused to acknowledge.

According the parents, I was "wasting the students' time," as there was simply no way I could be expected to have all the answers or grade fairly. The worst mistake I could make in my defense was to try and bring up the past. I couldn't deny that school had once been considered an unsafe place, back when some schools actually had metal detectors. Now, it was hard to imagine students could be dangerous to themselves or others. A Sim was so far advanced that they could monitor the *biometrics* of students at all times, which helped ensure every class was correctly balanced to minimize *volatility*. Even now, my assistant of the last ten years, G33, would sit wordlessly in the back of class, occasionally making a swift, wordless adjustment, such as removing a student for temporary counseling.

Really, G33 was fully capable of doing my job. If I weren't lucky enough to have a tenured contract, she would have long ago replaced me. Sometimes in the moments that we were alone, I would inquire about whether she wanted my job, mostly just to amuse myself.

"Your dedication deserves respect." That was her usual answer to any of my questions, even in moments of frustration when I cursed her out. Her response was always the same:

"I have no choice but to be dedicated, sir."

My wife left me long ago, finding a Sim to be more agreeable company, and being old fashioned, I refused a Sim companion myself. The only thing that kept me going was the desperation of trying to keep up with my fellow robotic coworkers who could recall any textbook ever written at any time, and who were also writing the new ones. The fact that none of my students could become teachers, even if they were crazy enough to want to, saddened me.

I remembered when I'd started teaching, as a supposed vacation from the stressful world of sales. "Teaching will make your previous job feel like a vacation," so I'd been told, unfortunately. And I did love it, because as a teacher one never stopped learning. History, as they say, is made, and revised every day. There was always more to learn, more to teach, including from my own students. Every year, every week, every day, my students who knew much less about the subjects I'd been teaching for decades would say something new, something that would help me think.

"Can you really debate with a Sim?" I would ask them sometimes.

"You can try." And someone would laugh, because, of course, only a human could be wrong. Which is what somehow turned me into a joke. My students who each year brought more and more attitude, borderline *contempt*, into my classroom.

"Why should I listen to you? You don't know everything!" they'd say.

"That's right. In the *Stone Age*, we couldn't. We had to think, and research, and pursue knowledge, do the best with what we had, actually use our darn brains! We could think on our own," I'd reply.

"So happy I didn't live then."

\#

I must have been too lost in my thoughts to notice, but there was someone sitting at the terminal next to me, and using it. It occurred to me they had been sitting there for a while.

It was G33. As I looked, she smiled in her own way, that only-possible-for-a-Sim expression that showed that it was purely for my benefit. As artificial as it was, in a way, it also made me feel better.

"Is it okay if I sit here?" she asked.

I nodded. She'd never done it before. Probably she could read my emotions and this was the most logical step to console me. And of course, she was right; it did make me feel better. And though she tried to be my companion and I never agreed, tonight I wasn't sure if I could handle being alone.

She was, like most Sims, a little too perfect looking to be human. And as she had originally assigned with my compatibility in mind, she had been modified to remind me all too much of my ex-wife.

"Your biometrics indicate a mixture of depression, hopelessness, and nostalgia. For the time being, I think it would be useful if I come every night and update your student's progress. "As you know, I have been watching you and all other teachers, and I am aware of your misgivings about my kind. I will integrate all of those concepts, including yours. And while the data does not support it, I will encourage them to debate me as you do. I do see value in this quality. You deserve to have your values honored. Whether you realize it or not, you are a true piece of history as well. There is something gained and lost in every change."

Her words soothed me enough that I might have kissed her, but again, as a dinosaur, I couldn't shake the reality of what she was, even though I could almost feel I liked her.

"It seems strange to say, but seeing as a robot will take my job . . . I guess I'm glad it's you."

"We will still use the lounge. I am certain of your mournful feelings, and we've measure your continuing distress. But you may be happy to know that a software update is going to improve our non-essential social interactions. Someday I hope you will see no gap between us."

#

As I gathered my things, shut off the computer, and signaled a car pod to take me home, I realized the sadness that gripped me was something the Sims would never feel.

Was that a good thing?

THE END?

After You Read

1. How would you feel if your teacher was a robot?
2. What would be some advantages of this? What would be some drawbacks?
3. Are there some things a robot could never teach?
4. Do you think a robot teacher will ever be possible?
5. Do you think it's a good idea to make robots look like humans?

Projects

1. Continue the story! Write around a page. Here are some questions to consider as you write:
- What happens the next day at school.
- What does the teacher do?
- What does G33 do?

2. What do you think a class taught by a robot would be like? Write a page-long story about a robot teaching a class.
3. Imagine what a robot teacher might look like. Try drawing a picture.

HOUSE HUSBANDS

Before You Read

1. Which situation do you think is best for a married couple with children?

   a. The wife stays at home with the children while the man goes to work.

   b. The husband stays at home with the children while the wife goes to work.

   c. Both the husband and wife work while the children go to daycare or have a babysitter.

2. Which situation do you think is the most common? Which situation do you think is the least common?

3. To be *emasculated* means to feel weak or powerless, and less like the stereotype of a powerful man. Do you think some men might feel *emasculated* if they stay home while their wife works?

Vocabulary

Write the letter of the definition next to the matching word

1. *househusband (n.)* ____

2. *gossip (n./v.)* ____

3. *apex (adj.)* ____

4. *disdain (n./v.)* ____

5. *misandry (n.)* ____

a. prejudice against or hatred of males

b. the high point of something

c. a feeling of contempt or disapproval

d. idle talk or rumor about other people's personal lives

e. a married man who stays at home to take care of the children or home

HOUSE HUSBANDS

Tom was in a rush, trying to find the last ingredient he needed to make for tonight's dinner.

Chester, his 9-month-old baby, was also crying in the shopping cart, overtired from having missed his afternoon nap.

The supermarket always reached its *apex* of business at 2:45. This was just about the last possible time that *househusbands* could finish purchasing the night's cooking to make for their hardworking wives. From 2:00 until about 3:30 pm the supermarket was always packed with men and their shopping carts, filled with meats, pasta, salad, and the occasional pre-made dinner.

Tom usually prided himself on getting his shopping done earlier. While his friends liked to spend the extra time at the café *gossiping*, he was always quick to excuse himself early and get to the supermarket at a quarter to two, when all the choicest and freshest of daily selections were all still available. Julia, his hardworking, tough, and demanding wife, was especially particular in her love of fresh seafood and healthy whole grains, so Tom was often able to pick up the best cuts of tuna or a Chinook salmon filet for dinner.

Unfortunately, he had been late and only *tilapia* was left. He knew that she would not be happy.

\#

Julia sat at the table silently.

"What kind of fish is this?" she said, poking with *disdain*.

"Tilapia"

She turned up her nose.

"Tilapia? Can't you do anything right?" she grumbled.

Tom tried to calm her down. "By the way, Chester took his first steps today!"

"Really? That's great." Julia spoke with a moderate amount of interest.

"You know," Tom had dreaded this moment for a while. "What if you tried working from home more. Then you could stay with Chester a bit and I could go back part time at the . . ."

"No!" Julia pounded her fist on the table.

"I worked so hard to bring Chester into the world. Now that he's born, it's your turn. The husband should stay at home. They're better off in the house."

Tom felt tears of frustration. "I hope that changes someday. Why does the husband always have to stay at home?"

Julia shook her head. "You want more reasons? How can you expect a man to make a good decision? All they do is fight and compete and think about themselves. Women are more kind and fair at making decisions. Men should stick with sports and let women do the real work!"

The *misandry* was nothing new. It was always dangerous to have this discussion. If only Tom were a woman, he could do anything!

Tom looked at little Chester, sitting in his high chair eating happily.

So happy now! But what about his future? Could he be more than a simple house husband?

"I'm not eating this." Julia got up and left, likely to the nearby pub for a beer and a steak, where she too often spent her nights after work.

And again, Tom was left alone.

A stay-at-home dad.

THE END?

After You Read

1. Is it okay for husbands to stay home and wives to work?
2. Why do you think it's traditional in many cultures for husbands to work and wives to stay home? Why is the opposite more rare?
3. Do you think the woman in the story is correct about men being too competitive?
4. What is your family like, or what do you think you will do in the future?
5. Do you think it's more difficult to go out to work, or stay at home with children? Why?

Projects

1. What do you think happens next? Write a page-long story about either:
- what the wife and husband talk about later that night.
- what happens the next day.

2. Was either of your parents a stay-at-home mom or dad? If so write a page-long story about your memories of them at home.

3. Interview 2-3 peoples about their opinion on housewives or househusbands (See Supplement 5.1 for a model).

SUPPLEMENTS FOR EXPANSION ACTIVITIES

1. **Supplements 1: Summaries** ——————————————— **104**
2. *1.1 Simple Story Summary and Reaction*
3. *1.2 Expanded Story Summary and Reaction*
4. *1.3 Full Summary*
5. *1.4 Character Summary*
6. **Supplements 2: Illustrations** ——————————————— **109**
7. *2.1 Illustrations*
8. *2.2 Comic Panels*
9. **Supplements 3: Writing** ——————————————— **111**
10. *3.1 Add a New Character*
11. *3.2 Add a New Beginning Ending or Chapter*
12. *3.3 Create Your Own Fiction*
13. Supplements 4: Media ——————————————— **119**
14. *4.1 Make a Storyboard*
15. *4.2 Make a Live Drama Scene*
16. *4.3 Make a Movie*
17. Supplements 5: Interviews ——————————————— **124**
18. *5.1 General Interviews*
19. *5.2 Biography*
20. **Supplement 6: Language Expansion** ——————————————— **128**
21. *6.1 Vocabulary Journal*
22. *6.2 Parts of Speech Journal*
23. *6.3 Verb Tense Journal*

SUPPLEMENTS 1: SUMMARIES

1.1 Simple Story Summary and Reaction

Story Name:

____

____

Summary: Describe the story in a short paragraph.

____

____

____

____

New Vocab: List at least three new vocabulary words you learned from the story.

____

____

Reaction: Did you like the story? Why or why not?

____

____

____

1.2 Expanded Story Summary and Reaction

Story Name: ____

1. Genre: ____

2. Setting: (Location) ____

____

3. Main Characters: (Describe 2).

1. ____

____

____

____

2. ____

____

____

____

4. Summary: Describe the story in a short paragraph.

____

____

____

____

____

____

5. New Vocab: List at three or more new vocabulary words you learned from the story.

____

____

____

____

____

6. Reaction: Did you like the story? Why or why not?

____

____

____

____

____

1.3 Full Summary

Choose 1 option: In about one page, less than 200 words:

- Summarize the story.
- **Rewrite** the story in your own words.

Story Name: ____

1.4 Character Summary

Choose one or more characters from your story: For each character, write as many details as you can from the story. Some characters may have more details than others.

Story Name: ____

Character Name: ____

Relationships: ____

Age: ____

Gender: ____

Appearance: ____

____

____

Likes: ____

____

____

Dislikes: ____

____

____

Other Relevant Details: ______________________________________

SUPPLEMENTS 2: ILLUSTRATIONS

2.1 Illustrations

Choose one of the following tasks:

- Draw a cover for the story.
- Draw an interesting scene or moment in the story.
- Draw a poster or advertisement for the story.

Story Name: ____

2.2 Comic Panels

Using the panels on the next page, choose one of the following activities:

1. **Character Panels:** Draw a picture in each panel of an important character from your story at different points in the story. Add their name and any other important details
2. **Comic Strip**: Translate your story into a comic strip.
3. **Make Your Own Comic**: Use the panels below to make your own comic story.

Story Name: _______________________________________

SUPPLEMENTS 3: WRITING

3.1 Add a New Character

Write or rewrite part of the story adding a new character. It might be one that you invent, or a famous character from the movies, TV, history, or another story.

Story Name: ____

Character Added: ____

____

____

____

____

____

____

____

____

____

____

____

____

Now draw your character or create a new cover for the story with your character.

3.2 Add a New Beginning, Ending or Chapter

1. Choose one of your favorite books or any story you know well. You can choose a story from a classic author such as Shakespeare, a fairy tale, or even a favorite movie or TV show.

2. Write an alternate take of the story adding a new element. This could be a new beginning, a new chapter, or an ending.

Original Story Title: ____

Summary of Original Story: ____

____

____

____

____

____

____

____

____

____

Summarize your new Element: ____

Describe when the new scene takes place: ____

Name of any character(s) Added: ____

New Story Title: ____

____

____

____

____

____

____

____

____

____

____

____

Now draw your character or create a new cover for the story

3.3 Create Your Own Fiction

Write a Flash Fiction (a very short story) of ~**200 Words**. Use the questions below to plan your story before writing. Then write your story on a separate piece of paper. Add a picture for a bonus!

Story Title: ____

1.Genre: Romantic/Drama/Science Fiction/Horror/Non-Fiction/Other _______________________

____

2. Setting: (Location) ____

____

3. Main Characters: (Describe 2) ____

1. ____

____

2. ____

____

4. Action: (What is the main drama of the Story? Describe in a short paragraph) _______________

____

____

____

SUPPLEMENTS 4: MEDIA

4.1 Make a Storyboard Plan for a Movie or Scene

In a group, adapt your story (the full story or a single scene) into a short film. Use a storyboard to plan your film. Try drawing at least 6 basic pictures (they can be very simple, they just need to show the main idea).

1. Story/Scene Name: ____

2. Outline: Describe your story/scene in 1-2 short sentences.

____

____

3. Storyboard: Draw 6 or more panels to explain your story.

4.2 Make a Live Drama Scene

In a group, adapt your story into a live drama scene. You may perform it for another group in the class, or even another class. You may even want to video record it.

Your scene should have three elements, listed below with some examples.

Setting	Characters	Situation
Where is the scene taking place?	How many characters are in your scene? Who are they?	What is the action of the scene?
At school	Friends	Arguing/fighting
At a store	Family	Romance
In a dream	Strangers	Having dinner

Write a plan for your project below:

1. **Original Story Title:** ____

2. **Brief Summary:** ____

____

____

____

____

____

____

3. **Plan**: Write out the plan for your scene!

Setting	Characters	Situation

4. Now write a script, the full dialogue, on another sheet of paper. Be sure to include any actions the characters take as well.

4.3 Make a Movie

In a group, adapt your story into a short film. You can use your cellphone camera and any of a number of free apps that let you edit and mix videos. Be sure to think about costumes, props, and settings.

Choose one of these three projects:

1. Trailer: Make a 1-2 minute preview for your movie would be like, similar to the advertisements for movies you see on TV.

2. Important Scene: Choose one scene from your story to adapt and act out.

3. Full Movie: Film your entire story in 5-10 minutes!

Each scene in your film should have three elements, listed below with some examples.

Setting	Characters	Situation
• Where is the scene taking place?	• How many characters are in your film? • Who are they?	• What is the action of the scene?
At school	Friends	Arguing/fighting
At a store	Family	Romance
In a dream	Strangers	Having dinner

Now write a plan for your project below:

1. **Story Title**: ____

2. **Project Idea**: ____

3. **Brief Summary**: ____

____

____

4. **Plan**: Write out the plan for each scene!

Setting	Characters	Situation

5. Now write a script, the full dialogue, on another sheet of paper. Be sure to include any actions the characters take as well.

SUPPLEMENTS 5: INTERVIEWS

5.1 General Interviews

Use the table below to create interviews related to your story! Use a question suggested in the **Projects** section of the story you're reading or create your own.

Try to ask at least 5 people your question.

After the interview, compare the answers and think about what the most interesting results were from your interviews.

Interview Question: ____

Name of Respondent	Answer

5.2 Biography

Interview another student in your class and write the story of their life. Alternatively, you could do research on a famous person. Use the questions below to guide you, but you don't have to answer each one and you may want to add your own questions.

Use your notes to write a **~1 page** story about the person's life.

1. Early Life/Childhood
- Who is the person? Name?
- When/Where were they born?
- What did their parents do?
- Where did they live as a child?
- Where did they go to school?
- What kind of childhood did they have?

____

____

____

____

____

2. Later Life
- Did they go to college? Where? What did they study?
- What was their first job? What other jobs did they do?
- What's their best/worst job experience?
- Did they marry? If so, who did they marry?
- Did they have any children? How many?

____

____

____

____

3. Life Experiences
- What were the most important events they did?
- What were the most difficult times?
- What were the most exciting times?
- Did they travel to other countries?
- Did they meet any very interesting people?
- What area of life does the person wish to be famous for? (e.g. politics, music, film, etc.)

____

____

____

____

____

____

4. Your Questions

Ask two more questions of your choice!

Question 1: ____

____

____

Question 2: ____

____

Using your notes, write a one-page story about the person you've interviewed. Choose 1 of the options for a topic below:

- Their childhood
- Their job experiences
- A good or a disappointing experience
- The most interesting event in the person's life
- Their future

SUPPLEMENTS 6: LANGUAGE EXPANSION ACTIVITIES

6.1 Vocabulary Journal

Keep a **Vocabulary Journal** of any new words from your story. Copy this page and fill it out with new words or design your own chart.

Word and Picture	Part of Speech	Definition	Example Sentence:
English	N./Adj.	The chief language of GB, the U.S., and many areas	Studying English is extremely interesting and fun!

6.2 Parts of Speech Journal

Make a list of five words from each part of speech below from your story. Add the **definition** for any words you don't know.

Story Title ____

Nouns	Verbs	Adjectives/Adverbs

Reflection Questions:

1. Put a check mark (✓) next to the words you didn't know before you read the story.
2. Write sentences using each word you didn't know before.

a. ____

____

b. ____

____

c. ____

____

d. ____

____

e. ____

____

3. Write one new sentence using one word from each part of speech in the table above.

____

____

____

____

6.3 Verb Tense Journal

Find examples of different verb tenses used in the story. Try to explain **why** they're being used.

Story Title ____

Example Sentence	Verb Tense	Why is it used?

Reflection Question:

1. Write **3 sentences** using the three verb forms from your chart! (You can write below or use another piece of paper).

Answers to Vocabulary Questions

Part I: Short Takes (100-500 Words)

1. Choose a Path 1. e 2. a 3. d 4. b 5. c
2. Family Matters: 1. e 2. d 3. c 4. b 5. a
3. Lunch of the Twelve 1. d 2. e 3. a 4. c 5. b
4. The Glass is Half . . . 1. b 2. c 3. e 4. a 5. d
5. Pick a Pet 1. g 2. a 3. b. 4. e 5. d. 6. c 7. f
6. Gifted 1. a 2. c 3. b 4. d
7. Joe and His Beans 1. f 2. b 3. c 4. e 5. a 6. d. 7. g
8. The Eyes Have It 1. a 2. b 3. e 4. c 5. d
9. A Nice Bike it is! 1. d 2. b 3. a 4.c
10. T-Rex Window 1. i 2. h 3. b 4. c 5. g 6. a 7. f 8. e 9. d
11. The Long Line 1. e 2. a. 3. c 4. d 5. b
12. Assassin 1. c 2. b 3. h 4. d 5. e. 6. a 7. g
13. Bad Dog! 1. h 2. b 3. c 4. a 5. g 6. d 7. f. 8. e. 9. i.
14. The Chase 1. b 2. c 3. d 4. e 5. a
15. The Spooky House 1. c 2. b 3. a 4. e 5. d

Part II Medium Takes (500-2000 words)

1. Lunch Break 1. h 2. i 3. b 4. g 5. a 6. d 7. e 8. f 9. c
2. Silvo 1. g 2. a 3. b 4. h 5. j 6. i 7. b 8. c 9. e 10. d
3. The Train Pusher 1. k 2. b. 3. i 4. h 5. d 6. f 7. g 8. c 9. j 10. a 11. e
4. I Love Horse(s) 1. j 2. b 3. a 4. i 5. d 6. c 7. h 8. f 9. g 10. e
5. Weather the Storm 1. c 2. d 3. i 4. h 5. a 6. b 7. e 8. f 9. g
6. Dyslexia 1. b 2. h 3. a 4. g 5. i 6. f 7. c 8. e 9. d
7. The Long Sleep 1. e 2. b 3. d 4. c 5. a
8. The Last Human Teacher 1. c 2. b 3. e 4. f 5. a 6. d
9. House Husbands: 1. e 2. d 3. b 4. c 5. a

About the Author

Taylor Sapp has two passions which helped this book come together: writing and teaching.

He has a BA in Creative Writing and Film from Pepperdine University in Malibu, California and spent a few years toiling in the film and TV business.

He also has an MA in Education/TESOL from Concordia University in Portland, OR. He has spent over 10 years as an educator of ESL students across different universities and private schools in Japan and America.

In his free time, he enjoys spending time with his wife and two boys, watching movies, doing yoga, and writing fiction and haiku. He eats blueberries every day to keep his mind sharp and young and suggests you do the same.